"The bright lights of London calling!"

Iain was clearly angry. "You can't wait to get back to them, can you?"

"It's nothing to do with bright lights," Susan protested. "But I have got my living to earn.... It's not that I *want* to go," she faltered. "I've...loved every minute of it."

"I know!" He gave her a grim nod. "It's all very quaint and amusing but not the sort of place you'd dream of for keeps."

"But there's no question of such a thing!"

"Of course there's no question of it," he said wearily. "I've realized that all along. But it's been so good having you here... and Jan."

His whole face softened as he spoke her name, and looking into his eyes Susan realized, *it's Jan. He's in love with Jan.*

ELIZABETH HOY

is also the author
of the following titles in
HARLEQUIN CLASSIC LIBRARY

For a free catalogue listing all available Harlequin
romance titles, send your name and address to:

HARLEQUIN READER SERVICE
M.P.O. Box 707, Niagara Falls, NY 14302
Canadian address: Stratford, Ontario N5A 6W2

Dear Fugitive

ELIZABETH HOY

Originally published as Harlequin Romance #573

HARLEQUIN
CLASSIC LIBRARY

TORONTO • LONDON • LOS ANGELES • AMSTERDAM
SYDNEY • HAMBURG • PARIS • STOCKHOLM • ATHENS • TOKYO

Original hardcover edition published by
Mills & Boon Limited 1960
ISBN 0-373-80037-1

Harlequin edition first published February 1961
Golden Harlequin Library edition, Volume XVIII, published August 1971
Harlequin Classic Library edition published December 1980

CHAPTER ONE

IT WAS breathlessly hot in Cromwell Gardens that August evening, and the air was heavy with the gas fumes shut in beneath a lowering London sky. Hurrying past the tall, shabby Victorian houses, Susan thought longingly of a cold bath. It would be bliss to have one before supper . . . if the bathroom was free—a matter of luck at Number Thirty-two, the apartment house where she lived in a modest bed-sitter, glorified by the name of "flatlet."

In the string bag on her arm a lettuce wilted. She had bought a slice of cooked ham to go with it, and a small carton of cream cheese. She'd eat early, she decided, put her feet up on her divan bed, read her new library book—and forget old Mr. Digby, who had been in one of his most trying moods today, because of the great heat, no doubt. He was well into his seventies and ought to retire, but there was no one to tell him so. As senior partner and chief shareholder he ruled supreme in the city office of Timber Imports Ltd., where Susan had worked for the past three years—in the general typing pool at first, and then as Mr. Digby's personal secretary, a promotion she usually enjoyed. But tonight she was tired . . . old Mr. Digby had really been impossibly captious, and never had the solitude and peace of her little apartment seemed more desirable.

With a blissful sense of release she ran up the steps of Number Thirty-two, slid her key into the hall door lock and let herself in, The communal telephone in its alcove beneath the stairs was ringing with ear-splitting insistence. Automatically Susan hastened to answer it, though she wasn't expecting a call herself and would probably be involved in a tiresome taking of messages for one of the other residents.

"Kensington, double one, two, double four," she murmured into the mouthpiece a little impatiently.

"May I speak to Miss Susan Harrowby, please?" a familiar voice demanded on an odd note of urgency.

"Mother!" Susan exclaimed joyfully. "How lovely to hear from you. I've just this moment walked in at the front door. Is everything all right at Moorings?" An unnecessary question—of course everything was all right at Moorings. She could see the quiet Sussex village as she spoke, and Sunnymead, her home, an old timbered house in a pleasantly casual garden—flanked by the church and vicarage, post office and general stores; right in the center of things, as a doctor's house should be. "I wish I were there at this moment!" she added nostalgically. "London is like an oven tonight—"

"Is Jan with you, Susan?" her mother interrupted sharply.

"No! Is she supposed to be?" Susan's heart missed a beat. Her mother, usually the most placid and sensible of women, sounded so shrill and peculiar—almost hysterical.

"I just thought she might have decided to stay with you last night . . . a forlorn hope!"

"You mean she wasn't at home last night, and you didn't know where she was?" Susan could hardly bring the preposterous question out. Jan, her seventeen-year-old, art-student sister was headstrong and impulsive, she knew, often wholly unaccountable and unreasonable in her actions, but she wouldn't, surely, be thoughtless enough to take herself off for a night without giving her parents some indication of her whereabouts.

And yet, apparently, that was exactly what she had done. "She went to her art class at Oakford yesterday morning," came the worried voice over the line, "and we haven't seen her or heard from her since." There was a muffled sound that might have been a stifled sob. "Most of her clothes have been taken from her wardrobe—Look, dear," Mrs. Harrowby broke off, "would you come home? Right away? Just for tonight? I can't very well explain it all to you over the phone. You could just about catch the 6:10 from Victoria. . . ."

"Of course, darling," Susan agreed breathlessly. "I'll start at once." Questions seethed in her mind, but already the line had gone dead. She hung up the receiver feeling as if someone had just hit her over the head. The whole thing was so absolutely fantastic! Jan missing from home—like some sensational character in a Sunday newspaper story, and her mother so agitated, so obviously alarmed that she was demanding Susan's return from London in the middle of a working week. This wasn't the kind of thing that happened to the Harrowbys! It simply didn't make sense.

Picking up her parcels, Susan made blindly for the stairs. If she was going to catch the 6:10 she'd have to hurry. Taking the three flights in a rush she arrived at her room breathless, threw the lettuce and ham and cheese into the minute fridge, collected toothbrush and night things, scribbled a note for the housekeeper canceling the morning's milk, and ran down again to leave the housekeeper's note on the hall table. Then with a fleeting regret for cold baths and library books she was out once more in the burning heat of the late afternoon. If she managed to pick up a fifty-three bus at the end of the road she'd just about make it!

In her rush to Victoria Station there was no time to think clearly. Conscious only of a nameless apprehension that made her heart beat uncomfortably fast, she fought her way through the home-going crowd of commuters, and fumed in a line at the ticket office. But safely at last in the train she drew a long breath and forced herself to survey the situation calmly. It was worrying, alarming even, but there was sure to be some simple explanation. If anything awful had happened to Jan, a street accident for instance—Susan shuddered—her parents would have been informed. Perhaps she had gone to an art-school party—a dance that went on later than she had expected—and she had spent the night, or what was left of it, at the house of a friend. But if so, she could have telephoned her home. And why had she taken her clothes? Little icicles of fear ran up and down Susan's spine. She opened an evening paper she had snatched from the newsstand on her way and stared blankly at the headlines. They might have been written in Greek for all the sense they made. Wild-eyed, she watched the parched summer fields slip past the carriage windows. Thank heavens it was a fast train; first stop Oakford, then Moorings Halt.

Half an hour later she was hurrying down the familiar flower bordered platform, avoiding the handful of passengers who had alighted along with her—commuting businessmen, a few housewives returning from a day's shopping in town—all of them known to her. Odd to find herself shrinking from them, terrified lest they might speak to her, ask awkward questions, wondering what was bringing her home at midweek. They knew she lived and worked in London. Like all people who dwell in small communities they had an uncanny knack of sensing the unusual and kept an eagle eye on the comings and goings of their neighbors. What a sensation it would be in the village if it were suspected that Jan Harrowby had disappeared! Which, of course, was completely crazy, Susan hastily assured herself. Jan *hadn't* disappeared. By this time the mystery would most probably have been cleared up. *I'll find she has got home before me,* Susan told herself stoutly, and looked around the station yard for her father's car. It was nowhere to be seen—he would be busy at his evening office hours, she remembered. She'd have to phone for a taxi or wait for the temperamental local bus. It was a good two miles from the Halt to the village center.

"Want a lift?" an unexpected voice hailed her. The open American roadster that pulled up in front of her was long, svelte, fabulous, a dazzle of cream and chrome upholstered in scarlet. And the girl at the wheel was as glamorous as her setting—blond, green-eyed, beautiful. Or she would have been, Susan had time to reflect, if she hadn't plastered quite so much makeup on her classic features.

"That's very kind of you, Miss Trent." Susan's tone was surprised and faintly distant. She hardly knew the girl, and the little she did know she didn't much care about. Sandra Trent just wasn't her kind—the spoiled only daughter of the blatantly new rich people who had recently bought Moorings Manor.

"Well, hop in, then." Sandra leaned over and opened the passenger door invitingly. Susan got into the car, still mildly mystified. Sandra Trent, full of herself and her own affairs, wasn't the sort to take pity on stray pedestrians.

"Were you expecting to meet somebody?" Susan asked as Sandra hesitated, her finger on the ignition switch, her glance raking the last straggle of passengers emerging from the station exit.

"I was . . . and I wasn't," Sandra drawled cryptically—and with an assumption of carelessness that somehow didn't ring quite true. "Actually, I came by on the chance of picking up Tony Brampton. But he obviously isn't there." She flipped at the controls and the great car shot forward at a speed that might have been alarming if it had not been so seductively smooth.

"He went up to London yesterday to an art show, and from what he said I rather gathered he'd be returning tonight. But he's so frightfully vague about everything." She broke off with an exasperated sigh. "You don't happen to know when he *is* coming back, I suppose?"

"Why, no!" Susan murmured, dumbfounded. What had Tony Brampton's movements to do with her? She'd never even spoken to the man—a famous society portrait painter who had been staying in the village at the Amberhurst Arms. According to local gossip Sandra had met him on a recent visit to Paris and persuaded her father to commission him to do her picture. But that was weeks ago. The portrait must have been finished long since. What then was keeping Brampton in the district? Sandra's charms? Or her wealth? Or a combination of both? Susan couldn't have cared less.

"It just occurred to me," Sandra was saying, "that your young sister, Jan, might have gone to the same show."

Susan colored, aware that the hooded green eyes were watching her narrowly. But it was idiotic to come across all hot and bothered at the mere mention of Jan's name. "I really wouldn't know," she said woodenly.

"Well, she has gone to some sort of art show," Sandra persisted. "I saw her yesterday morning when I was collecting a package from the left luggage office. Jan was withdrawing a suitcase—which seemed to me a bit odd. I mean, she must have deposited it the night before for some reason of her own. She told me it contained canvases she was taking up to a student's exhibition.'' She looked at Susan piercingly. "Didn't you know she was exhibiting in town?''

"No,'' Susan returned flatly, hiding her astonishment at the news of Jan's trip to London.

"You'd think she'd have told you,'' Sandra mused, then shrugging the unimportant detail away, "Anyway, it wouldn't be the show Tony was going to—I mean, kid's stuff, student's efforts—the sort of thing that bores him stiff. And Jan no doubt would have come home last night.'' Once more there was that piercing questioning glance. Susan said nothing.

"When Tony goes to a show it has to be something outstanding,'' Sandra went on. "Usually it is abstracts . . . terribly modern stuff. The kind of painting that attracts only the avant-garde.'' She brought out the French phrase with a self-conscious flourish. "People like Topolski and Francis Bacon. Tony knows them all and when he goes up to town he invariably gets involved in dinners and cocktail parties . . . has a job to tear himself away. It might be a week before he shows up again.''

Susan offered no comment, having no interest whatever in the artistic dallyings of the unknown Brampton. But it all sounded rather as if Sandra were trying to convince herself of something, whistling in the dark. There was a brief, uneasy silence; Susan's thoughts were busy with the puzzling item about Jan. That suitcase she had so mysteriously left in the luggage office overnight . . . containing canvases, she had said. But it had also no doubt carried the clothing missing from her wardrobe. Where had she been going to? And why all the secrecy? It was all so improbable—and so worrying! The more she tried to work it out the more puzzled Susan became . . . and all the time she was aware of Sandra flinging her those odd little watchful sidelong glances.

Presently she said, "You're the eldest Harrowby girl, aren't you? The one who works in London. You don't come home very often?"

"Usually only at holiday times," Susan agreed, "and for an occasional weekend—when I'm lucky enough to get a Saturday off. I work for an old-fashioned boss who doesn't believe in five-day weeks." *And what on earth has it got to do with you*, she longed to add.

"How foul for you!" Sandra was murmuring sweetly. "But you have managed to get home this evening. Is it a birthday, or something?"

"No," Susan returned coldly. "It isn't." If it sounded like a snub she didn't care. Sandra Trent was really being impossibly inquisitive, but they had reached the gate of Sunnymead, Susan saw with relief. She was out of the big, showy car almost before it had stopped, flinging a perfunctory, "Thanks for the lift," over her shoulder as she ran up the garden path.

Her mother, waiting for her at the door obviously on the watch, glanced curiously at the car as it drove away. "Was that Sandra Trent?" she asked in a tone of amazement.

"She happened to see me at the station and offered to drive me home," Susan explained.

Mrs. Harrowby's brows shot up. "Most unlike her to be so neighborly." She looked gray and worn, her eyes dark shadowed, as though she had spent a sleepless night.

"How quick you've been getting home, darling. I can't tell
you how glad I am to see you!" Her welcoming kiss had an
odd intensity. Susan saw her face quiver as she turned
away. "Let's go and sit down and I'll tell you what it's all
about. . . ."

With an abstracted air she drifted into the drawing room
that opened out of the hall, and Susan followed her. The
bright homey room seemed to radiate comfort—and
peace. The familiar Aubusson carpet with the worn spot by
the hearth, the deep chintz-covered chairs, the late roses in
a silver bowl on the low central table, it was all so much as
usual. Susan breathed an unconscious sigh of relief.
Nothing could go seriously wrong at Sunnymead—nothing
ever had. It was home, it was love and security; all the dear
foundations upon which her young life had been built.

"What was she doing at the station?" Mrs. Harrowby
was asking, still apparently harping on Sandra Trent.

"Does it matter?" Susan murmured. Surely she hadn't
come home to discuss Sandra Trent! "She said she had
been half-expecting that artist friend of hers to turn
up. . . ."

"Tony Brampton." Mrs. Harrowby nodded with a kind
of grim satisfaction. "It all ties up, I'm afraid. He wasn't
there, of course?"

"No, he wasn't. Sandra said he'd gone up to town
yesterday to see an art show. . . ." Susan broke off with an
impatient gesture. "But what on earth has all this to do
with Jan?"

"That's what we are trying to find out," Mrs. Harrowby said. Her eyes, fixed desperately on Susan, were
suddenly filled with terror.

"She didn't go to her art class at Oakford yesterday

morning," Susan said. "Sandra Trent saw her catching the London train . . . taking a suitcase out of the left luggage office. . . ."

Mrs. Harrowby gave a queer little wounded cry. "I knew it! Oh, Susan! This confirms our worst fears. Tony Brampton may or may not have gone to a London art show yesterday, but wherever he went we think Jan was with him. She has run away with him, Susan!" The last words were hardly more than a whisper.

Susan sank weakly into the nearest chair. "Oh, mother . . . how awful! Are you sure?"

"Everything points to it." Mrs. Harrowby moved nervously around the room, picking up a fallen rose petal, straightening a cushion.

"I . . . wasn't even aware that she knew him," Susan said incredulously.

"She met him at the art school last term." Mrs. Harrowby subsided limply onto the settee. "He had been invited by the principal to criticize the students' work, and he seems to have been impressed by Jan's talent. That started it all, I suppose. You know how seriously Jan takes her painting?"

Susan nodded. For a moment they gazed at one another in bleak silence. Jan with her disconcerting streak of genius—had they ever known her without a pencil in her hand? "Obsessive drawing," Dr. Harrowby called it. But the drawings were so good. She had fought her way tempestuously through her schooldays, hating every part of the curriculum but the weekly art session. If she had knuckled under to the drudgery of general studies in the end, it was simply because a graduation diploma was necessary to her main purpose. She had wanted to try for a scholarship at the Royal Academy School, but her parents had refused to hear of it. She was too young at sixteen to leave home and mix with a Bohemian crowd of young painters, they had declared, and must content herself with a year at least at the nearby Oakford College of Art—a small but competently run establishment affiliated to the local technical school. If the principal at Oakford thought her work promising they would think about a London training for her later. . . . Had they been wrong to curb her ambitions? Self-doubt flickered across Mrs. Harrowby's worried, kindly face.

"But Anthony Brampton!" she cried out to Susan appealingly. "A painter with an international reputation. Could she have met anyone more likely to rob her of every shred of her native common sense? She was wax in his hands. He talked to her of Rome, of Paris, loaned her books on old masters . . . and new; invited her to the studio he has rented in Oakford. Can't you imagine how all this went to her head?"

Once more Susan nodded wordlessly. In the deep soft chair she felt small and cold and singularly helpless; dreading the climax of the story, yet wishing her mother would hurry along with it.

"When she said she was going to have private lessons during the long summer vacation," Mrs. Harrowby resumed, "we naturally concluded she would be having them from that Miss Blakely, the Oakford College art teacher who has given her extra tutoring from time to time. I'm afraid she rather misled us about this—not that she tried exactly, but she certainly concealed the fact that it was at Brampton's studio that she would be painting. It didn't come out until the other day—and by then it was too late for us to do anything about it. By then she was head over heels in love with Brampton . . . and he with her. He came to your

father one day last week and announced that they wanted
to be married—straightaway.''

"Gosh!" Susan murmured inelegantly, on a surge of
relief she did not care to examine too closely. But a dread
too hideous to be put into words had been lifted from her
heart. "It could have been worse," she said. "He might
not have been the marrying sort!''

"I know!" Mrs. Harrowby shuddered. "But it was all
so ridiculous, Susan. Jan is only seventeen. Brampton
must be close to thirty, and a pretty sophisticated thirty at
that, a rootless, cosmopolitan type, with no home but
some kind of ramshackle studio in Paris. He had to get
back to France, he declared, the atmosphere in England
stifled him. People were so deadly dull and uninspiring. It
wasn't exactly a tactful approach, was it?" She laughed
mirthlessly. "Anyway, it went on and on . . . he must
return to Paris and Jan must go with him. They were vitally
necessary to one another. They must live and love and
paint together. . . . In the end your father quite lost his
temper, I'm afraid, and ordered Brampton out of the
house.''

"Why couldn't they have been engaged?" Susan ventured.

"Oh, Brampton didn't believe in engagements. When
two people were made for each other—as Jan and he
were—there was no point in waiting around. Love was too
precious to be put into cold storage, was one choice little
epigram I remember. They could, he announced, be married by special license in a few days. . . . It was at this point
poor old dad exploded.''

"I don't blame him!" Susan sympathized.

"As if we would consider for one moment allowing Jan,
at her age, to go rushing off with this man of whom we

knew nothing—save that he came here in the first place to dance attendance on Sandra Trent, who, by the way, quite obviously regards him as her personal property and is, no doubt, livid with Jan for annexing him.''

"Do you think she suspects they have . . . eloped?" Susan choked a little over the word.

"I imagine so. Hence her interest in your arrival at Moorings this evening."

"She certainly did her best to pump me about Jan's whereabouts," Susan mused.

"How did Jan take it when dad sent Anthony Brampton packing?" she asked after a momentary pause.

"She . . . shut up like a clam. You know how she is when she is hurt—silent and elusive, keeping out of the way. Mostly she stayed in her room, painting. Dad had forbidden her to see Tony or to communicate with him. She seemed oddly submissive over that. I was so relieved, fool that I was, telling myself the whole thing would blow over," Mrs. Harrowby shook her head at her own credulity. "We were specially gentle with her, thinking she was suffering from heartache, never dreaming it was hidden defiance and bottled up excitement that was making her so pale and distraught." Tears filled Mrs. Harrowby's eyes. "It didn't occur to me that she was getting up at seven—an unheard of hour for Jan—in order to waylay the mailman. Not even when I came down one morning to find her hurriedly slipping an envelope she had taken from the mailbox into her pocket did I suspect the truth. Tony, we found out later, had been writing to her daily . . . planning their elopement, I suppose." Mrs. Harrowby buried her face in her hands. "Oh, Susan how could she have been so cruel and deceitful? What we went through last night waiting for her to come in!"

Susan slid onto the settee and put a comforting arm around her mother's bowed shoulders. "She didn't mean to be cruel, darling. She just didn't think. She's so young and . . . impulsive, and this man has swept her off her feet. I'm sure it is because he is a famous painter that she has lost her head over him so completely. When she discovers he is just another selfish artist, far more interested in his own work than in hers, she may give up the whole thing—and come home."

Mrs. Harrowby straightened up and wiped her eyes. "No, Susan, she won't come home. I *know* Jan. The more snags she runs into, the more obstinate she will become. She'll get her own way if it kills her. She has always been the same. I remember when she was a little thing of five, a nursemaid we had locked her in the bathroom for punishment, because she was teasing baby Bridget. She thrust her fat little arm right through the glass door, found the key and let herself out—dreadfully cut and bleeding. Your father had to put several stitches in the wounds, but she didn't cry—she didn't care—she had got her own way and that was all that mattered. It is the same blind, mad courage and willfulness that has sent her off with this man Brampton."

"You're quite sure she *has* gone to him?" Susan hazarded in a shaken voice.

"Where else can she be?"

They gazed at one another in a despairing silence that seemed to ache and throb with all their unspoken fears.

Then the door opened and the youngest Harrowby daughter came in—fourteen-year-old Bridget, blond and plump and placid, a younger edition of her mother. Susan—tall, slim, fair-skinned and gray-eyed—took after her long-legged, aquiline father, but Jan resembled neither of her parents. Jan was a law unto herself—dark-haired, dark-eyed, vivid in coloring as a sun-warmed apricot. There was a touch of the exotic about her, for though she was taller than Susan she had a sinuous grace and was oddly mature in figure and looks for her age. A throwback, they said, to a Sicilian great-great-grandmother, who had been brought back to England as a bride by an eighteenth-century Harrowby making the grand tour. Mysteries of heredity . . . could the sultry temperament of that long ago Sicilian bride have anything to do with today's tragic little drama? In the welter of speculation seething through Mrs. Harrowby's mind, the question hovered for an instant—farfetched, remote, scarcely acknowledged.

"Oh, Susan, you have come home! How super!" Bridget's jaunty air was a little forced, and her glance went uneasily to her mother's grave and anxious face. "Is it because of . . . Jan, Susan is here? Is there any news yet?"

Mrs. Harrowby drew in a sharp breath, but her voice was resolutely bright saying, "No, dear, we haven't heard anything so far. I phoned Susan this afternoon and suggested she should run down for the night to help us decide what to do. . . ."

"Not that I'm being much use, I'm afraid," Susan said weakly. Her mother turned to her with a quivering smile. "Just having you here to talk to is wonderful, darling!"

Bridget absently twirled the tennis racket she was carrying. Her blue eyes, fixed on Susan, were round and bright with awe. "Do you think we will *ever* hear from Jan again?" she hazarded in desperation.

"Of course we will," Susan declared robustly.

"Maybe they'll come back and see us—when they are married," Bridget went on with it. "That is if dad forgives them." She gave a small shaken laugh. "Imagine us having an elopement in the family—and Anthony Brampton for a brother-in-law! I played a ghastly game at the vicarage this afternoon—couldn't keep my mind on it . . . thinking about Jan. It was an awful job not to let it all out. I'm sure Mr. and Mrs. Roborough and the girls suspected something.''

"Nonsense!" Mrs. Harrowby put in sharply. "How could they possibly suspect anything?"

But sooner or later the scandal of Jan's disappearance would be all over the village. Already, it was clear, Sandra Trent had a pretty shrewd idea Tony Brampton was involved.

Throughout supper the Harrowbys discussed the situation—distractedly, helplessly. Until they had some idea where Jan had gone there was so little they could do. By this time she might be in Paris. . . .

Dr. Harrowby, coming late from a heavily attended evening practice, was tight-lipped and grim. He had been so proud of his beautiful, clever Jan! Long ago, without any resentment, Susan had guessed at his special affection for his second-born child. Perhaps because she had given him more trouble than either of the others he had loved her best. The wound she had dealt him now would go very deep.

"If she doesn't make some sign of life by tomorrow we will have to contact the police," he declared with an off-hand gruffness that deceived nobody.

"She'll write," Susan urged. "I'm sure she will soon let us know where she is."

"We don't want the police mixed up in it unless we are absolutely forced," Mrs. Harrowby shuddered. "Think of the hideous publicity! Jan would be marked for life."

"It would get into all the papers," Susan groaned.

"Tony Brampton, the society portrait painter, is quite a celebrity in his way. I can just see the headlines: 'Seventeen-year-old art student elopes with famous artist. Irate father in hot pursuit. . . .' "

Dr. Harrowby's thin sensitive face went a dull purple. "If I could just get my hands on the bounder! Working on Jan's love for her painting . . . luring her away with heaven knows what false promises of fame and glory—a most ingenious line in seduction!" He stood up with a goaded air. There were one or two sick calls still on his list, he said, and after that he would be at the cottage hospital if they wanted him. "I have a difficult confinement to cope with tonight," he warned his wife. "Better not wait up for me." As he strode from the room his shoulders sagged, his brief mood of bombast deserting him. He looked pitifully vulnerable now—and utterly defeated.

Hollow-eyed, Mrs. Harrowby watched him go from the room. "This is breaking his heart," she said in a low tone as the door closed behind him.

Susan began to clear the table. "He has eaten scarcely anything. It's all wrong . . . hours of hard work still before him. . . ."

"I'll leave a thermos of hot milk and some sandwiches in the office for him," Mrs. Harrowby said. "That is if I go to bed before he comes in. I never felt less like sleeping."

"But you must, mommy, darling," Susan urged in loving concern. "You look absolutely all in! It won't help things if you collapse for want of rest."

Somehow they got through the endless evening. Every time the phone went they started up, pale with apprehension. But invariably the calls were for the doctor—a neurotic old lady reporting a "queer spell of dizziness," a mother with a teething baby who wanted to know if she might safely give a mild dose of sedative. Mrs. Harrowby, who knew as much about teething babies as any doctor, was able to offer helpful advice. And the doctor, she promised, would look in in the morning. To the dizzy old lady she made a similar promise.

"Tell her," added Bridget, toying listlessly with a jigsaw puzzle, "to take more water with it!"

At eleven o'clock they all went up to bed, shepherded by an adamant Susan. In her dressing gown a few minutes later she slipped back to the kitchen to heat a cup of milk, which she insisted upon her mother drinking with a couple of aspirins. "There will be a letter from Jan in the morning," she declared with more force than conviction. "You'll see, darling! I'm certain she'll write."

"And if she doesn't?" Mrs. Harrowby inquired bleakly. "You'll stay on, won't you, Susan? You won't leave us until this dreadful uncertainty is past?"

"Of course I will stay," Susan promised, resolutely thrusting the thought of the exigent Mr. Digby out of her mind. It was agonizing to see her usually calm and practical mother so tremulous and dependent! Had Jan the faintest idea of the misery she was causing her parents? For hours Susan lay awake, torn between indignation at her sister's thoughtlessness and compassion for her folly—rushing off into the blue with this unknown man . . . cap over the windmill! With one wild impulsive act Jan had thrown away her carefree girlhood. Wrecking her youth . . . if not her whole life, Susan thought drastically. And however it turned out things would never be the same again for any of them. The peaceful pattern of family life had been shattered. The old easy days of happy companionship and unclouded trust were gone forever. Jan had broken faith with them. Something infinitely precious had been destroyed.

As she turned and tossed on her bed through that endless night, Susan's eyes were wet with tears. Jan had gone from them—cruelly, mysteriously. And Jan—as she had been—would never return. It was as if she had suddenly become a different person . . . almost as if she had died.

CHAPTER TWO

SLEEPING FITFULLY at last, Susan woke early. For a moment she lay dazed, while the events of the previous day seeped gradually back into consciousness. Things were bad enough, but the black mood of the small hours had evaporated. Jan had gone off with Tony Brampton. With the resilience of youth Susan was able to face the fact more equably this morning. If it was a fact. After all, weren't they rather jumping to conclusions? Perhaps Jan had done no more than make a secret trip to London to enter her pictures for an exhibition . . . meaning to surprise the family with the awards she hoped to win.

But it wasn't a very convincing supposition.

Susan heard the garden gate open on squeaking hinges and the rattle of the mailbox in the hall as the postman deposited the morning mail. She scrambled out of bed and threw on her dressing gown. But already her mother was hurrying up the stairs, and as Susan opened her bedroom door she called out that the mail had come . . . bringing a letter from Jan.

She sounded incredulous and shaken, and without waiting for Susan's comment darted into the room where her husband awaited her. The door swung to behind her. Susan listened to the muted murmur of urgent voices from behind the closed door—feeling a little shut out and hurt.

But almost at once her mother called to her, "Susan, come here, dear!" It was impossible to tell from her tone if the news from Jan was good or bad. But at least she had written.

Heavy-eyed, vaguely headachy after her broken night's sleep, Susan hurried into the big familiar bedroom. Sunlight streamed in through the wide bay window. She blinked in the glare, and saw her father in pajamas and dressing gown, the shaving lather wet on his cheeks. He was holding a single sheet of notepaper in his hand, and his frozen immobility struck a chill at her heart. He looked like a man who had suffered a mortal blow.

"Well, at least we know the worst now!" Mrs. Harrowby announced grimly. In her trim cotton housecoat she seemed oddly composed—her hair freshly done, her face pale but serene. "At all events the child is . . . alive . . . and well!" The sigh of relief that escaped her revealed the possible horrors imagined, the fears that had been set at rest. Taking the scrawled sheet of paper from the doctor's hand she passed it to Susan.

Susan stared at it stupidly for a moment in a haze of apprehension, then steadying herself with an effort she read the hurriedly penciled lines. It was Jan at her worst, immature, cruel and triumphant. She wrote:

We are in Scotland, Tony and I, where people can get married at seventeen if they want to without any silly fuss about parental consent. We've merely got to stay here three weeks to establish residence. Then we will be married. Please don't follow us or try to find us, because you never will and it would be a complete waste of time and effort. Our minds are made up, and I know we are doing the right thing. One day, I am sure, you will agree it was all for the best.

"She gives no address, of course," Mrs. Harrowby pointed out. "But the envelope is postmarked 'Edinburgh.' " She picked it up from the bedside table and extracted another small fold of paper. "Mr. Anthony Brampton's contribution," she announced dryly.

Susan unfolded it gingerly, feeling a little sick. But on the whole, it was a more adult, more considerate communication than Jan's childish scrawl. He was sorry things had to be this way, Tony wrote, and he begged Dr. and Mrs. Harrowby not to think of him too hardly. Susan read aloud in a deadpan voice.

It is imperative for my work that I should get back to Paris as soon as possible, and neither Jan nor I believe in needless separation, as I tried, unsuccessfully, to make you understand. My one concern, as I still hope you may come to realize, is for Jan's happiness. I will, I assure you, take care of her in every way. At the moment, there is nothing more I can say. I can only ask you to trust me, forbear with me—and believe me.

Yours sincerely,

Anthony Brampton

"The gall of the man!" Dr. Harrowby exploded. "You must go to Edinburgh at once, Susan, and bring Jan home. Your mother and I have been talking it over and that is the decision we have come to. It is impossible for me to leave my patients, single-handed in the practice as I am, and with the household affairs to see to and Bridget's winter school term looming, your mother cannot very well be spared."

"Besides," Mrs. Harrowby put in before Susan had time to protest, "we think you would probably have much more success with Jan than we would. She thinks the world of you—looks up to you—you could talk to her in the language of your own generation—whatever that language may be. It seems to be something we don't understand," she added bitterly. "After all we said, all we had to say to her about Tony Brampton ten days ago . . . and this," she ended hollowly, "is the result! So, Susan dear, I do think you should go and see what you can do."

"But Edinburgh," Susan gulped. "It's a huge place. Where would I begin to look for her? And then there is my job. . . ."

"I'm sure Mr. Digby would give you a few days off if you explained that you wanted it for urgent family reasons."

"No need to be explicit with him," Dr. Harrowby added warningly. "The fewer people who know of Jan's disgraceful behavior, the better. The one thing we've got to avoid is unpleasant publicity—for Jan's sake . . . for all our sakes!" He took a roll of bills from his wallet on the dressing table. "This should see you through a week. I'll let you have some more later on, if you need it. . . ."

Susan looked at the money indecisively. "It seems such a wild-goose chase," she offered doubtfully. "Even if I find Jan, which is highly unlikely, she'll never agree to abandon Tony and come meekly home. You know how determined she is. . . ."

"Tell her," said Dr. Harrowby grimly, "that I, too, can be determined. There are legal steps I could take to prevent this marriage. An expensive and distasteful procedure . . . I hope she won't force me to it. We can try reasoning with her first."

Mrs. Harrowby threw Susan a terrified glance. "You *must* go to her, Susan! Make her understand. . . ."

"If only I knew how to set about looking for her!" Susan said.

"Inquire at hotels; go to the registrar's office," Dr. Harrowby advised. "Couples intending to marry surely have to lodge some kind of formal notice with the authorities."

"Supposing they have gone farther afield than Edinburgh?"

"I don't think they'll have done that. A small place wouldn't be so easy in which to hide." The doctor picked up a towel and wiped flecks of drying lather from his chin. "I'll finish dressing and run you to the station. The main thing is that you should start off with the least possible delay."

"Breakfast is ready," Mrs. Harrowby put in. "You'll just have time to pack a few things while I make the coffee."

"You can be in town by nine. See Mr. Digby and catch the morning express from King's Cross," Dr. Harrowby declared firmly as he vanished into the adjoining dressing room. Mrs. Harrowby had already hurried off to see about the coffee.

They weren't leaving her much choice, Susan thought. Rushing her off in this hectic fashion. But they were desperate, poor darlings. If it helped them to feel she was wandering around Scotland trying to find Jan it was up to her to get on with the hopeless task. At the moment it seemed to her an utterly fatuous undertaking.

Returning to her room she stuffed woollies, a change of undies and a couple of cotton dresses into her lightest suitcase. She had never visited Scotland before; it would be exciting to see the beautiful city of Edinburgh. Arthur's Seat, and Holyrood, the castle on its mighty rock above the green slopes of a fabulous garden—pictures she had seen ran vaguely through her mind. Princes Street with its beautiful shops, the old town where through the stormy centuries the Stuart kings made history—if only she were going to discover it all in happier circumstances! With an involuntary shudder she came back to earth. Surely dad hadn't meant those horrible things he had said about seeking legal aid? It all sounded so unlike him. But he was distracted with anxiety over Jan—and he loathed Anthony Brampton. Could he really be the monster her parents seemed to imagine him to be? Susan found herself wondering. Dimly she remembered having seen him in the village post office, earlier in the summer—a large, untidy-looking young man with a pleasantly absentminded manner and a certain air of distinction. She had thought him quite attractive. A sneaking sympathy for Jan stirred in her heart. It would be a heady experience for a girl of seventeen to have a man like that in love with her. She herself had never been seriously in love, but in the depths of her heart she believed that one day it would happen to her—and when it did, it would be for all time. A romantic idea perhaps, but when she met her man she would know him at once—without any doubt. Love, it seemed to Susan, though she could hardly have put it into words, wasn't only a physical attraction, but a deep and abiding truth that beckoned once in a lifetime—a passing of angels' wings in the dusty mortal byways. Was it something like that for Jan and her Tony?

"Your coffee is waiting!" came her mother's voice sharply from the kitchen. Susan closed her suitcase with a snap and ran downstairs.

HALF AN HOUR later she was in the London-bound train, on the first lap of her strange questing journey. At Victoria she took a taxi, extravagantly, to Cromwell Gardens to leave a note for the milkman and newspaper man, and to tell the housekeeper she would be away for a few days. Then she went on to the office, hoping Mr. Digby would have arrived. He had and answered her request for a leave of absence with a point-blank refusal. She had had her annual summer holiday, he reminded her. They were busy. He couldn't imagine any crisis in her affairs being more urgent than his own need of her, and, anyway, why couldn't she say outright what this mysterious crisis was all about?

"It's . . . a private matter, Mr. Digby," she faltered. "My parents are in difficulties over a family matter, and only I can help them."

"Is somebody ill?" he demanded.

"No," Susan told him, feeling more and more uncomfortable. "It's not exactly an . . . illness. I promise you I won't be away longer than I can help."

The veins on Mr. Digby's aged brow swelled alarmingly. "I'm not interested in your promises!" He banged on his desk with an emphatic fist. "Let's have no more of this nonsense, Miss Harrowby. You're not having any time off. I can't spare you. And I want that report on Riga Incorporated typed out before lunch."

"Miss Woods is already doing it," Susan assured him, speaking of her very efficient junior. "She is quite capable of handling my work as well as her own for a short period. Please, Mr. Digby— I *must* have a few days off!"

"All right!" Mr. Digby blazed. "Take all the days you want. Take the rest of your life, as far as I am concerned. For if you leave my office this morning, you leave it for good. Understand?"

Susan swallowed an angry lump in her throat. "I quite understand. But I still have to go. I'm . . . sorry." She turned and walked to the door, where she halted and looked back inquiringly. Surely Mr. Digby wasn't serious!

"Get out!" he roared.

Bitterly resentful, Susan went on her way—unceremoniously sacked—after three years of faithful service. It was unreasonable, unfair. . . . In the outer office Linda Woods offered hurried words of comfort. Mr. Digby was crazy, half-gaga, a miserable old tyrant too long accustomed to having his own way. "People his age hate having their little ways upset. Before the day is over he'll regret what he has done and be wishing he had you back."

"I daresay he will," Susan agreed bleakly. "But I can't wait around for him to come to his senses. I've got to catch a train to the North." She threw a hunted glance at the clock on the wall, aware that Linda was watching her curiously, bursting with curiosity. Ignoring the charged atmosphere, Susan handed over the keys of her desk, issued a few last minute instructions, and murmured a flurried "goodbye."

A moment later she was whirring down to street level in the familiar elevator. She couldn't believe she was using it for the last time—flung out on her ear—jobless! Timber importing was a pretty specialized business. For three years, indeed ever since she had left school, she had been learning all there was to know about it. And it looked as though all that painfully accumulated knowledge was going to be wasted. She wouldn't easily get another post as private secretary to a director in the same trade. So it would mean starting at the bottom with some other kind of firm, working again as a typist probably in some vast impersonal pool.

On the crowded pavement she stood dazed, suitcase in hand. First the wretched upheaval of Jan's elopement—and then this! With a feeling of worlds crashing around her, she hailed a passing cab. "King's Cross as quickly as you can get me there," she told the driver. Throughout the brief ride she sat on the edge of her seat, watching the traffic lights. Strung up as she was, the catching of this particular train seemed to her all-important. Unspecified urgencies hounded her. If she could only reach Edinburgh while Jan was still there! In spite of what her father had said it seemed to Susan quite possible that the runaway lovers might decide to move on.

When she got to King's Cross there was just time to buy her ticket and race along the platform to the waiting train. Doors banged, a whistle sounded. Hampered by her suitcase, her handbag and the coat she was carrying, she clutched ineffectually at the handle of the nearest compartment door. The train was actually on the move when a pair of strong hands seized her by the shoulders and lifted her bodily into the carriage.

"That was a near thing! Here, let me take your case. . . ." The voice had a pleasant Scots' burr to it, and glancing up, shaken and bewildered, Susan found herself looking into a pair of dark hazel eyes—half amused, half concerned and wholly friendly. They belonged to a tall, loosely put together young man in a countrified tweed suit.

She watched him hoist her case onto the rack above the one vacant seat remaining—the corner window seat opposite his own.

"You'll need to get your breath," he remarked sympathetically as she sank down, gasping. "That was quite a sprint you put on down the platform. I never thought you'd make it!"

Susan managed a flustered smile. "I wouldn't have done—without your help. Thank you for coming to the rescue."

"Think nothing of it!" The hazel eyes twinkled. "Glad I happened to be on the lookout."

If you hadn't been, Susan thought with a shiver, *I might well have been under the wheels.*

Settling in his corner, the young man unfolded a morning newspaper. Covertly, Susan glanced at his lean, muscular hands. Her shoulders still ached from their purposeful grip. But everything about him, she noticed in that first swift survey, was lean and muscular and purposeful. Close-cropped dark hair with a hint of curl in it, a jutting well-cut nose and dogged chin—his skin was burned to an Indian red brown with wind and weather—an outdoor type, forester perhaps, or farmer. Idly she summed him up, idly dismissed him, the anxieties she had thrust aside for a preoccupied moment crowding back on her once more, like pain that returns after the brief respite of sleep. In the hours ahead, cooped up in her railway carriage corner, she would have all too much time to think. Turning to the window she gazed unseeingly at suburban back gardens and wondered with cold foreboding what lay in wait for her at this strange journey's end.

CHAPTER THREE

THE HUM of the wheels had a hypnotic effect. Resting her head against the stiff railway upholstery, Susan closed her eyes . . . and instantly saw Jan's vivid lovely little face, clear as a colored photograph imprinted on her lids. Where was she at this moment? What was she feeling? Was she lonely . . . beginning to be afraid of the decisive step she had taken or, more characteristically, defiant, triumphant, enjoying her adventure without a qualm? And where, in the end, would that adventure lead her? Away from her home, her parents, her friends to an unknown world in which she would be utterly dependent on Tony Brampton for her happiness. Supposing he failed her? Susan repressed a shiver. *I've got to find her*, she thought in sudden almost unbearable urgency: *talk to her, reason with her . . . before it is too late.* They had always been so close to one another in spite of the four years difference in their ages. They had shared dreams, plans, confidences. And it hurt now that this supreme confidence—Jan's first serious love affair—had not been shared.

If I had been at home more often this summer she might have told me about it, Susan reproached herself. But she had spent her holidays on a walking tour in Cornwall with a group of friends from the office, members of a Ramblers Club to which she belonged. Almost every fine weekend had been devoted to the club's activities.

Systematically they had explored the highways and byways of the more accessible home counties . . . while Jan, deprived of her most natural confidant, sensing perhaps her parents' inevitable disapproval, had gone her secret way, getting herself more and more deeply involved with this man who had walked into their lives out of the blue. *If only I had met him a couple of times, so that I'd have had at least an inkling as to what he is like,* Susan thought. But she had been too busy with her own affairs to keep in touch with Jan's doings. Tears were suddenly wet on her lashes; she felt them roll down her cheeks and furtively wiping them away, opened her eyes to find the young man opposite watching her. He glanced away at once, of course, his lean brown face rigid, as though he were embarrassed at the sight of her distress. Holding his morning newspaper wide open, he hid himself effectively behind its capacious pages.

Susan glared at the paper barricade, unreasonably annoyed at the awkward little encounter. She was tired with emotional strain. She had slept so little last night—her nerves were all on edge, and the more she thought about it the more doubtful she was about the wisdom of her journey. Tearing off after Jan with no clue to her whereabouts but a postmark. If her parents hadn't been half-mad with worry they would never have advocated so hopeless an enterprise.

At Peterborough three people got out of the carriage. Susan had a momentary wild impulse to follow them— take the next London-bound train and go home. But while she was still debating this cowardly retreat a mother with a baby got in and by the time Susan had given the woman a hand with her various bundles the train was once more in motion. The baby, a lively two-year-old, jogged up and down on its mother's knee, chortling with delight at the sound of the wheels. Susan and the mother exchanged smiles and a little desultory conversation. It was wee Caroline's first time in a train, the mother announced. They were going to Grantham to visit the child's grandmother.

The young man in the corner rustled his newspaper. Susan without turning her head knew he had put it down. With the slightest encouragement he would, she felt, have joined in the conversation. Indefinably she resented this . . . annoyed with herself for her awareness of him. But ever since he had helped her into the train it had been there—a sort of vibration in the air—a magnetic current tugging at her attention. As if, in some mysterious way, he was refusing to be ignored and kept out of her thoughts. But she was imagining things, she told herself, and heard with relief the inviting tinkle of the luncheon bell. She would go along to the restaurant car, she decided; treat herself to a slap-up meal. It would help to pass the time—and she was, she discovered, ravenously hungry. After all, she had had breakfast at half-past seven—a good five hours ago.

Making her way along the swaying corridor she could hear firm footsteps close behind her. Her nerves gave a premonitory tingle, and she was scarcely surprised to find a swinging door being held open for her by the young man from the corner seat. Inevitably, they entered the crowded dining car together, to be pounced upon by a white-jacketed steward who put them at the only available table: a small table for two. So that once more they were opposite one another, this time inescapably linked by the exigencies of a meal shared at close quarters. In a flurry that was not altogether unpleasurable, Susan dropped her napkin. The young man retrieved it and handed it to her with a smile.

She could do no less than return that smile—and thank him.

Soup came, swaying in shallow bowls.

"Storm in a soup bowl," the young man said. "Why do trains always seem to put on an extra spurt of speed and instability just as one reaches the dining car?"

"But meals on a train are fun," Susan said, and surprisingly meant it. She hadn't thought anything could be fun on this journey, but suddenly her spirits had unaccountably lightened. The soup was good, sunlight danced on the white tablecloth, on sparkling glass and cutlery; beyond the window at her side harvest fields, orchards and woodlands unrolled—and the quizzical brown face confronting her promised an hour of pleasant companionship. To have repulsed the friendliness offered would have been ungracious and ridiculous. Instinctively Susan knew this young man was not the type to presume on a travel acquaintanceship. And in an odd way it was a relief that the silence between them had been broken—that odd magnetic pull. All along they had wanted to talk to one another, but hadn't known how to begin. Not that it mattered a great deal, Susan hastily assured herself. It was quite unimportant—one of those casual contacts so easily made in a railway train and just as easily forgotten.

"They do a very good grilled turbot on this train," he was saying, studying the menu.

"Do you often travel on this line?" Susan asked.

"Not very often, once or twice a year when business takes me to London. This time I went to see an exhibition: farming machinery and fertilizers and so on—agricultural gimmicks mostly." He offered the mildly derogatory term with a grin.

So she hadn't been far-out in her guess at his profession.

"Mechanics and chemistry," he said. "You have to be a bit of a scientist these days to keep up with it all."

"Mechanics and chemistry," she repeated. "It doesn't sound a bit like farming."

He grinned. "And how do you think farming ought to sound?"

She pondered a moment, and smiled. "Slow going and tranquil—the lowing herd winding slowly o'er the lea . . . and all that sort of thing."

"I'm inclined to agree with you . . . But you've got to compete with the get-rich-quick boys if you want to succeed, give nature a shot in the arm to speed her up and hustle the lowing herd into mechanical milkers. The modern farmer is all out for high profits and quick returns—synthetics poured into the soil, calves bred from test tubes, poultry in battery installations. Some of it is all right of course . . ."

"But not the birds in batteries," Susan said quickly. "I saw them on television once, and I thought it all looked quite horrible. Those poor hens shut up all their lives in little dark boxes . . . never able to scratch around. They can't be happy."

"They aren't," he agreed. "But the money rolls in."

Susan went on with her turbot in silence, her gray eyes troubled. It was silly to feel disappointed because a man who was a total stranger seemed all at once a bit hard and inhuman. "Unhappy hens," she murmured doubtfully, "they must lay unhappy eggs."

He burst out laughing. "You're absolutely right. Though I've never heard it put quite like that. But nothing will persuade me that mass produced eggs have the same food value as eggs produced by the slower, old-fashioned way with free-moving birds. Personally I wouldn't touch the battery method with a barge pole."

Her long lashes lifted. The quick look she gave him was curiously intense. "You'd rather lose money?"

"Much rather."

She felt an odd little pang of relief.

"Not that we bother much about poultry nowadays," he went on. "But the birds we do have run free. Kirstie looks after them. Kirstie, by the way, is my sister. Keeps house for me. . . ."

So he lived with a sister . . . not a wife. And it couldn't, Susan reminded herself, have mattered to her less. In a few hours they would go their separate ways—he to his farm— in some Highland fastness, she imagined; she to the friendless blank of an unknown city. In a swift engulfing flood all her worry came back to her. With a suppressed sigh, she turned to the window—factories now instead of orchards, rows of back to back houses instead of fields. Mountains of slag towered beside a pit head, whole ranges of somber cone-shaped peaks. "Is that how a coal mine looks?" she marveled. "I don't believe I've ever seen one before."

"It's your first trip North, then?" her companion remarked.

"Yes, I'm going to Edinburgh."

"For the festival, I suppose."

"The festival?" She stared at him blankly, then her memory clicked. "Oh, yes, the famous Edinburgh Festival. It begins this week, doesn't it. I'd forgotten all about it, I'm afraid." She wrinkled her fine brows in their characteristic little frown. "Edinburgh will be pretty crowded, I suppose. It won't be easy to find anywhere to stay tonight. . . ."

"Bit risky chancing it this time of the year." His tone was mildly puzzled. "You haven't made a reservation anywhere?"

"No, there wasn't time. I came away in such a hurry."
She looked down at her plate. Plum tart now and whipped
cream, but her appetite had suddenly deserted her. Why
hadn't they remembered about the festival? Edinburgh
would be filled with visitors—tourists, foreigners of every
nationality. A seething mob in which Jan and Tony would
so easily be lost, and not a hotel room to be had for love or
money. She could see herself tramping the streets all night,
lugging her suitcase. She put down her spoon and fork, her
face pinched and tight, her lips tremulous—not quite
under control.

"Forgive me . . . but you're in trouble of some kind,
aren't you?" The voice from the other side of the table was
very kind. "I couldn't help noticing it . . . just after you
got into the train at King's Cross."

Those telltale tears, she remembered. Her cheeks went a
faint shamed pink. "People often cry in trains, for one
reason or another," she said with a small shaken laugh.

"And your reason?" he prompted gently. "Would it
make things any better to talk about it? Please don't think
I am being inquisitive, but if there is anything I could do to
help . . . at least I might be able to suggest somewhere you
could stay. . . ."

"Do you know Edinburgh well?" she countered, playing for time.

"I live about eighteen miles south of the city, but I'm
going straight through to Waverley Station now. My car is
waiting for me in the garage there. I'd gladly run you
around to one or two hotels when we arrive. . . ."

"It's very kind of you." She gave him a quick, uncertain
glance. "You must think me an awful clod not to have
reserved a room. But it just didn't occur to me. My mother
and father didn't think of it, either. We were all in such a

flap this morning. . . .'' Should she go on with it? The dark hazel eyes watching her were warm with sympathy and oddly concerned.

Taking a deep breath, Susan plunged. "It's my young sister. We're madly worried about her. She has . . . run away to be married—to a man my parents don't approve of. She's only seventeen.'' Her voice trailed away. It sounded a banal enough little story, told badly like this. Once more she hesitated.

"And you think she may be in Edinburgh,'' the young man prompted.

"We had a brief unsatisfactory letter from her this morning, just saying they were in Scotland, but giving no address. The envelope bore an Edinburgh postmark.''

"So you rushed off and took the first available train North.''

Was there a hint of mockery in his tone? But the lean, brown face was grave and serious, the hazel eyes bright with sincerity. Looking into their depths Susan felt reassured. There was an air of good sense and complete honesty about this man. If he offered advice it would be carefully considered. And it would, it occurred to her, be illuminating to have a disinterested opinion on the problem of Jan's marriage. See how it struck someone completely outside the family. Suddenly Susan found herself pouring out the whole story with astonishing ease. Her parents' anxiety for Jan, their dislike of Tony, their determination to stop the marriage at all costs and their inability to leave home.

"So they sent me.'' She made a small helpless gesture. "With only a postmark to go on. I haven't a clue where to begin looking for my sister. . . . She may have left Edinburgh by now, for all I know. If ever there was a more hopeless errand!'' Her gray eyes were dark with distress. ''And it has cost me my job in London.'' She told him then about old Mr. Digby—tetchy, unreasonable, bad tempered with gout. ''Acted as if I was an office boy asking for a day off to go to a nonexistent grandmother's funeral. Told me in no uncertain terms that I could clear out . . . and I did. With no reference, no word of appreciation . . . not even my week's salary. And all that after three years' hard work. Is it any wonder I was looking a bit the worse for wear when I flung myself into the train at King's Cross?''

He shook his head in commiseration. ''No wonder at all! You've certainly got quite a row to hoe, one way and another.''

''And it isn't as if I knew a single soul in Edinburgh.''

He leaned across the little table persuasively. ''You know me. At least I hope you will! Name of MacDowell, Iain—very much at your service.'' He gave her a quaint little bow.

The swift color ran up her cheeks. ''It's very good of you . . . but . . . .''

''I'm merely a rather pushful character you met on a train.'' The hazel eyes twinkled. ''And you'd like to know something more about me. You're perfectly right, of course.''

Susan laughed. ''That wasn't at all what I was thinking. What I was going to say when you interrupted me was that there really isn't very much you can do. Come to that, there isn't much I can do myself. The chances of my tracing my sister are pretty small it seems to me, and I've got a feeling my efforts are doomed to failure. To please my parents I can make inquiries at a few hotels, drift around the streets for a couple of days in the hope of running into Jan and Tony, and my father suggested a call at the registrar's . . . to find out if they were likely to turn up there sooner or later to apply for a marriage license, or whatever it is people have to do when they marry outside a church.'' Her voice trailed away on a discouraged note. ''I've no idea what the Scottish marriage laws really are.''

Iain MacDowell's lean face lighted up. ''I have an uncle who may be able to advise you about that. In fact I'm certain he can . . . marriage regulations should be right up his street. He is a lawyer, has quite a large practice in Edinburgh, and I wouldn't mind betting he knows exactly what runaway couples do when they come to that city. He has probably handled dozens of cases like yours. I'd gladly introduce you to him, if you like.''

''Oh, but that would be wonderful!'' Susan's voice was quite quavery with relief.

Iain gave her a compassionate glance. ''A bit of a thing . . . sending a girl of your age off on a job like this,'' he murmured indignantly. ''Your parents must have a lot of faith in you.''

''There was nobody else to send,'' Susan said simply. ''And I'm not perhaps as young as you imagine. I'm twenty-one . . . and the eldest of the family.'' Unconsciously she squared her shoulders. ''Naturally I'm the one my parents depend on the most.''

''Are there many of you?''

''Just Jan . . . the runaway, and a school-age sister, Bridget.''

''And your own name? You haven't told me that yet.''

Susan gave it to him with a smile. ''Susan Harrowby.''

Iain MacDowell sketched another little bow and his white teeth flashed in a quick warm smile. ''Glad to meet you Miss Harrowby . . . and I'll be still more glad if our meeting results in my being able to do anything to help you iron out some of your problems. To begin with I can stick around this evening, until I've made sure you have found somewhere to stay. We could try the hotels near the station first, and if there're all full there is a festival office just off Princes Street where they hang a board outside giving a list of recommended guest houses and private hotels with accommodation to spare."

For a moment Susan could only gaze at him in wide-eyed gratitude. Edinburgh no longer loomed as a vast unfriendly vacuum. She would arrive there with an escort . . . someone who, odd as it might be, really seemed to care what became of her. And there was this uncle person in the background who knew all about runaway couples and would advise her what to do about Jan.

The steward was bringing the coffee now. She poured it out—heartening and fragrant. "I can't tell you how I was dreading my arrival in Edinburgh. . . . It all seemed so hopeless and vague. But now . . ." she broke off with a tremulous smile.

"Now," he echoed with a nod and a grin, "you can sit back and relax. Let the Clan MacDowell take over!"

They lingered over their coffee, chatting easily. They might have known one another for years, Susan found herself thinking. The barriers that normally exist in the early stage of an acquaintanceship simply weren't there. And Iain talked well, with a touch of Gaelic eloquence, his Scottish intonation increasing as he described the whitewashed farmhouse on the slopes of the Grampians where he has spent his childhood.

"The Grampians . . ." Susan put in. "That's the place that always seems to turn up in the weather reports with the first winter snow. People go skiing there, don't they?"

"The idle rich, perhaps," he laughed. "There wasn't

much time at Bencramond for winter sports with five hundred sheep to tend. In the lambing season it was a twenty-four-hour-a-day job. Sometimes a whole week would go by when my father and I never got a chance to take off our clothes. We'd just snatch an odd hour of sleep on the settle by the kitchen fire."

His mother, she gathered, had died when he was a small child. Kirstie, his sister, apparently a good deal older than himself, had brought him up. The farm was isolated; it was a hard and lonely life for the three of them. National service and two years in sun-drenched Cyprus had made him realize how bleak were the conditions under which they had lived. He had come home just in time to see his father die of bronchial pneumonia brought on by exposure. Rounding up his sheep one January night he had been overtaken by a blizzard and, lost on the mountain side, he had all but perished before a search party rescued him.

"It's a bonny country up north, but a cruel one," Iain went on. "Though we loved our home in those grand, wild mountains, we somehow couldn't abide it anymore after our father's death. So we sold up and came south." He had wanted to be done with sheep he said, but he didn't know much about general farming and had thought of taking up market gardening. Then they had found Glenelg on the fringe of the Lammermuir country—an old Georgian mansion in a state of disrepair, "going for a song." The land surrounding it was fallow and rich and there were low hills where he could still keep a few sheep. It was Kirstie who had insisted upon the sheep. She said they would tide him over until he could establish himself with his fruit and vegetable growing. The great walled garden on a southern slope was an ideal place for him to make a start. It was five years now since they had moved in.

"And you're making a success of it?" Susan said. Somehow she couldn't see Iain MacDowell with his homespun good sense as a failure.

"We're not doing so badly," he admitted. "But it hasn't been easy going. The house was practically falling apart. We've been getting it to rights gradually, with the help of a couple of local handymen, decorating one room at a time when we could fit it in with the outside work. But there's still plenty to do and we haven't yet been able to afford to have electricity installed. Our one consession to modern comfort is a telephone. In winter we light our living rooms with oil lamps and candles and warm them with huge log fires, kept going with the dead wood I'm still cutting out of the surrounding woodlands."

Log fires, oil lamps, walled gardens—the pleasant picture conjured up seemed to take Susan miles away from her own gnawing troubles. "Glenelg," she said wistfully, "sounds like a haven of peace."

He gave her an oddly speculative look. "But you'd find it dull, I'm thinking, after your gay London life. Theaters and cinemas," he said, "concerts on your doorstep for the taking. Do you ever go to the proms at the Albert Hall?"

They talked about music then. She was surprised how knowledgeable he was ... in spite of that lonely farmhouse on the slopes of the Grampians. "What I know I learned by listening to the radio programs," he told her. "I never missed a prom if I could help it. I used to hear the youngsters on opening night, clapping and stamping, chanting "We want Malcolm!" until the maestro himself appeared. I can tell you I envied them! I used to picture it all down to the last detail . . . the lights and the flowers and the music. . . ."

She could see him, lonely and eager and young, famished

for life and color, coming in out of the gray mountain mists to sit on the fireside settle and listen to the great symphony orchestra playing four hundred miles away—Bach, passionless and cool as a sunrise, Beethoven with his triumphant affirmations, Mozart, spontaneous as rippling mountain water, tragic and joyful.

He belonged to a musical society in Edinburgh now, he told her. "Mostly," he said, "we concentrate on Scottish folk music and dancing, but we have our classical evenings as well. And here I am talking about myself again!" He gave her a half-shamed glance. "The trouble is you are far too sympathetic a listener. Believe it or not, I'm the tongue-tied sort as a rule, haven't unbuttoned like this for years!"

She was absurdly gratified. "But I've loved it," she assured him. "Every minute of it."

When they went back to their carriage the mother and baby had gone. They sat in their corners, reading and talking at intervals. Iain had produced the *Farmer's Weekly* from a capacious pocket and handed the daily paper over to Susan. An article on irresponsible teenagers brought Jan sharply back to her mind. Edinburgh was drawing near; the pleasant little interlude in the train began to shrink. So soon now it would be over.

They were just about over the border, Iain announced presently. "Like to come out to the corridor window and have your first glimpse of Scotland?" he suggested.

In the racing train they stood side by side, looking out at the placid sunlit land. There were glimpses of the North Sea, steel gray and cold even on this August afternoon, but landward the corn was golden and the Lammermuir Hills a soft velvety blue. Iain pointing vaguely to the west said Glenelg was not far away as the crow flies. "But not being a crow I have to go through to Edinburgh and prosaically pick up my car." There was an eager, home-going note in his voice that made Susan feel suddenly lonely again.

She said, "It's going to delay you, I'm afraid . . . bothering about me and my hotel."

"It will be no bother at all," he assured her, but his tone was a little absent, his mind and his interest already, she thought, hurrying away from her to the busy life awaiting him in which she had no part.

At Waverley Station it was all bustle and confusion. Iain had what he referred to as "clobber" to collect from the baggage car. Rose trees done up in sacking, a drinking trough for the hens and presents for Kirstie, Susan gathered. The car, when they got to it, proved to be a roomy station wagon.

Princes Street was at its late-afternoon liveliest. The castle, high on its bastion of rock, had a solid, uncompromising air, faintly menacing, so that the trees and flower garden in the deep valley beneath it seemed incongruous—like children dancing in the shadow of prison walls. Susan looked at the crowds thronging the pavement before the row of elegant shops. Fewer people walked on the garden side of the street, she noticed. She wondered what she should do if she were suddenly to see Jan, and unconsciously began to scan the passing faces with panic in her heart.

They tried three hotels, only to be turned away. "It's just as I feared," Iain said. "The center of the city is packed. Let's go and find that notice board." But when they got to it, it was to discover that the few guest houses with rooms to spare were situated far away in the suburbs.

Iain read them out in a discouraged voice. "It's going to

take a whale of a time to get around that lot," he said. "And we've no guarantee you would have a night's lodging at the end of it. Ten chances to one, some other benighted traveler will have been there before you."

I really am being a nuisance, Susan thought bleakly. *He wants to get home.* She said hurriedly, "I'd better try them, all the same, but you've wasted enough time over me already—I can take a taxi."

He gave her a long pondering glance—as if he wasn't listening to her. "Look—" he put an urgent hand on her arm "—why don't you pack it up for this evening, and come out to Glenelg with me? Kirstie would be only too pleased to give you a bed—"

"Oh, no!" Susan interrupted in genuine horror. "A blank stranger walking in on her out of the blue . . . she'd think it most odd. It's terribly kind of you, Mr. Mac-Dowell, but really I couldn't impose on your sister to that extent."

"You wouldn't be imposing. And the name, by the way, is Iain." He smiled down into her anxious upturned face. "Come on!" he urged boyishly. "You're tired and it's late. You can start room hunting first thing in the morning if you like. I can bring you in by car when I come in to Edinburgh with my fruit and vegetables. I make an early round of my customers every morning."

He was edging her purposefully toward the waiting car as he spoke. She could feel the pressure of his strong lean fingers on her arm. His nearness confused her.

He said in a bantering tone, "If you're afraid I'm some murky kidnapper we can drive around by Uncle Hamish's office and ask him to give me a character reference."

"No, no," she laughed. "There was nothing like that in

my mind—it was just that I hate being such a trouble to you . . . and your sister.'' But she was already in the car, the door slamming at her side.

They were nosing through the tangle of traffic when Iain spoke again. ''You're not being a trouble,'' he said. ''If you want to know . . . I'm glad you couldn't find a room.''

CHAPTER FOUR

IT WAS A RELIEF to leave the city behind. Susan watched the
suburban houses thin out, giving way to hedges and fields
and an occasional farm. Drowsy with a mild travel
headache, she felt a little bemused. Here she was driving
off into the blue with a man who was a complete stranger—but didn't seem like one. The hours they had shared
in the train had, in retrospect, an odd quality of
timelessness. Was it only this morning she had left home?

They had turned off the main road now into a network
of lanes lined with hazel bushes and bright-berried rowan
trees. Iain drove in silence, with a preoccupied air. Perhaps
he was wondering how he would account to his sister for a
stray young woman picked up on the train. "A penny for
your thoughts," Susan ventured.

He gave her a sideways glance, and laughed. "If you
must know, I was thinking about my dungle-dozer."

"Your *what*?" Susan demanded, wondering if she had
heard aright.

"My dungle-dozer—a Heath-Robinson agricultural con-
traption that is the light of my life—mixes compost. I
loaned it to a chap who keeps a turkey farm near my place,
and he phoned me just as I was leaving for London the
other day to say the engine had stalled. I've got to go
around there tonight and see what he has done to gum up
the works: popped a couple of paving stones into the mixer

I expect. Ham-handed type—hasn't a clue about machinery, but he provides me with invaluable fertilizer all the same . . . turkey droppings!'' There was a yearning note in his voice. "You've no idea what that sort of stuff, properly processed, can contribute to the soil.''

"How interesting,'' Susan murmured encouragingly. She liked the way his lean face lighted up as he talked.

"You see, I'm trying to do almost entirely without chemical fertilizers. I'm one of the back-to-nature boys where vegetable growing is concerned, fruit too, of course, grain, root crops the lot. A man who produces food for the open market has a big responsibility on his hands. But I'm boring you. . . .''

"I'm not in the least bored,'' Susan declared with truth. "I think it's fascinating. I'd no idea a market gardener could be a . . . sort of crusader.''

"People buy and eat anything they see in the shops. It's up to the producer to do their thinking for them; see they are given what's wholesome and 100 percent nourishing. Modern methods for stimulating the soil are all right in some cases, but you have to keep a wary eye on them.''

"Even if it means giving yourself extra work, making compost and so on.''

"Exactly. You're an understanding girl, Susan . . . that's what makes you so good to talk to!'' The sidelong glance this time was so warm with commendation that she went a little pink. And he had called her Susan: in the most natural way in the world it had slipped out.

The lane dipped and turned. "When we get around the next corner there's a gap in the trees through which you can get your first glimpse of Glenelg,'' Iain told her. A moment later Susan saw the big white house in its saucer-shaped valley, low beech-covered hills rising behind it.

"It's beautiful!" she cried spontaneously. "Tucked into the landscape as if it had been there for generations . . . almost as if it had grown there of its own accord."

He gave a little nod of agreement. "That's what comes of expert planning. It was built in 1775 under the influence of the famous Adam brothers. They were Scots, you know, hailed from these parts—sons of an Edinburgh architect. You'll find their porticos and molded ceilings and exquisite fireplaces cropping up in all sorts of unlikely places in the Lowlands. We've got quite a selection of them at Glenelg."

"And yet you picked it up for a song!"

"Because it's one of those rambling old houses no one wants to live in anymore. But Kirstie and I like it fine."

An understatement, Susan felt—there was a glow of sheer love in his voice.

The lane had degenerated now into what was little more than a rutted cart track. The station wagon rocked from side to side; Iain didn't seem to notice. A hump-backed bridge took them over a singing peat-colored burn, and a moment later they were passing through a pair of beautifully wrought-iron gates into a leafy driveway. Susan found herself tense with expectancy as they rounded a curve and the great house stood before them. She had a swift impression of an imposing facade, a noble sweep of shallow steps leading up to a pillared portico—and then the hall door opened.

The woman who stood on the threshold was tall and thin, her graying hair drawn severely back from her brow. Older than Susan had vaguely envisaged her, but unmistakably Kirstie. She had the same heavily lashed hazel eyes as her brother, the same high cheekbones and obstinate line of jaw. But the strong, shapely bone struc-

ture that made for good looks in Iain were in her case too
sharply defined, giving her a haggard air. If she had been
plumper it might not have been so noticeable, but there
was no feminine softness to help her. Flat-chested,
angular, dressed in a washed-out shrunken sweater and
dowdy tweed skirt that did nothing to flatter her figure,
she stood looking down at the car in a grim, uncompromising way. A woman who would ask no quarter of life—and
give none. Dour, was the adjective that flashed into
Susan's mind. She began to feel distinctly nervous.

"You're late," Kirstie called out, with no hint of
welcome, as Iain emerged. "I was beginning to wonder if
you'd missed your train. . . ." She broke off with an audible gasp, catching sight of Susan. Iain opened the
passenger door for her, a look of secret amusement on his
lean brown face. Quite clearly he was enjoying Kirstie's
astonishment.

"I caught the morning express all right," he drawled,
taking his time over it, deliberately prolonging the
suspense. "And we made good time from London. But I
delayed a while in Edinburgh, helping Miss Harrowby here
to search for a room. The hotels, however, are chock-full
with festival visitors . . . so I brought her home."

"So I see," Kirstie remarked dryly.

Susan advanced to the foot of the steps and stood hesitant. This was dreadful! She ought not to have come.

"Miss Susan Harrowby . . . my sister, Kirstie Mac-
Dowell." Iain made the formal introduction with a touch
of defiance. As if he were flinging the two women at one
another and challenging them to make the best of it.

"How do you do, Miss MacDowell?" Susan murmured
in an agony of embarrassment.

Kirstie seemed to be swallowing a lump in her throat.

"How do you do, Miss Harrowby?" She held out a hard, thin hand as Susan came up the steps. "Any friend of Iain's . . ." she began in a bewildered tone.

"We . . . met in the train," Susan faltered.

Kirstie's jaw dropped . . . almost audibly.

"I hadn't remembered it was festival time," Susan went on desperately. "Your brother warned me on the way that it might be difficult to find accommodation, and when we got to Edinburgh he very kindly drove me to several hotels, but they were all full. So he suggested I should come here . . . just for the night. I do hope it won't put you out too much."

Kirstie ignored this cue for polite reassurance. "Have you come all the way from London?" she asked.

"Yes, I left home in rather a hurry . . . there was no time to make arrangements. . . ." *It sounds as though I'm escaping from the police*, Susan thought, with a wild desire to giggle. She looked around in desperation for Iain, who with masculine unconcern was unloading the luggage from the car. Why couldn't he have stood by her and helped her with her explanations, Susan wondered indignantly. Perhaps he was already regretting his impulsive action in bringing her to Glenelg. She was mad to have agreed to it!

"I got you those rose trees you wanted, Kirstie," he was saying, coming up the steps. "And a most ingenious water trough for the poultry yard." He put Susan's suitcase down at her feet. "I'll take the rest through to the back," he announced, and promptly returned to the car and drove away.

Kirstie picked up the suitcase. "This will be yours, I suppose, Miss Harrowby. I'll leave it here in the hall for now. I've no room fit to show you into at the moment, but I'll make up a bed for you after we've had supper." She led the way across a wide circular hall, the rounded walls soaring in uninterrupted grace to the galleried floor above. It was lighted by a domed glass ceiling, high overhead. The ornate staircase, branching as it swept upward had the frozen beauty of a leafless tree. An impressive entrance, but hardly homely. As they crossed the black-and-white-tiled floor their footsteps echoed emptily.

"I do feel apologetic about bursting in on you like this," Susan murmured uncomfortably.

Kirstie's automatic, "Not at all . . . you must just take us as you find us," was polite. Nothing more.

They went down a dark corridor into a large bright kitchen with a cheery red-tiled floor and an old-fashioned, open-fire cooking range on which an array of saucepans simmered; geraniums bloomed on a deep windowsill where a gray tabby cat lay curled in sleep. It was all very cosy after that rather awe-inspiring hall.

"We live mostly in the kitchen to save work," Kirstie stated simply.

"It's a very charming kitchen," Susan offered—and hoped it didn't sound too patronizing.

There was an awkward pause while Kirstie peered into the saucepans on the stove. "If you'd like to freshen up after your journey," she said, "there's a washroom just along the passage on the left-hand side." She went over to the table and began to rearrange knives and forks. "I'll need to lay another place," she remarked grudgingly, or so it seemed to Susan, who colored painfully.

"Look, Miss MacDowell," she began with nervous emphasis. "I ought not to have come here. It is most unfair on you. Your brother suggested it without thinking—out of sheer good nature, because he saw I was in difficulties.

Isn't there a village inn or even a farm cottage in the district that would put me up for the night?"

"No, there isn't," Kirstie declared in her uncompromising fashion. She glanced at Susan's troubled face and added more genially, "Don't look so worried! You're welcome to stay here—if you don't mind things being a bit rough and ready." Her lips twitched and a slow smile broke over her grim features. Then, to Susan's surprise, she burst out laughing. "If you only knew how funny it is . . . Iain, the girl shy, walking in with a strange young lady! I was fit to drop when I saw you getting out of the car." She shook her head incredulously and went off into another peal of laughter. "If I seemed a bit slow to welcome you, it was because I was so taken aback."

"Well, naturally you were," Susan agreed, and went several shades pinker. And it was just at that moment that Iain appeared at the scullery door with an assortment of packages in his arms. "What's the joke?" he inquired.

"I think I'll go and have that wash," Susan mumbled in confusion and fled.

The washroom was white tiled and spotlessly clean, and the water running into the wash basin beautifully hot. It was bliss to be alone for a moment, washing away the grime of the journey, recovering her equilibrium. As she brushed her hair Susan could hear a murmur of voices from the kitchen. Iain, she hoped, was by now adding his explanations to her own—appeasing the formidable Kirstie. Though she wasn't quite so alarming when she laughed . . . saying Iain was girl shy. Was he? She wouldn't have thought it, Susan mused. He had managed their growing acquaintanceship on the train with a quiet assurance that had made it all very easy—too easy, perhaps. Talking to him she had almost forgotten poor little Jan. *If I had stayed in Edinburgh this evening I might already have run into her,* Susan thought guiltily. But it was a pretty remote chance. In the morning she would be rested and better able to work out some plan of action . . . with the convenient Uncle Hamish to help her.

She wondered if she ought to phone her parents and let them know where she was, but decided to wait until tomorrow when she would have a more permanent address to give them. In the glass above the mirror her face looked small and peaked, her eyes too large, bright with strain and shadowed with fatigue. Absently she dabbed powder on her small straight nose, touched her lips lightly with color—and returned to the kitchen-cum-livingroom feeling a little more able to cope with the redoubtable Kirstie. She was putting a succulent leg of roast lamb on the table and brusquely invited Susan to sit down. Iain sharpened the carving knife. The cat uncurled itself from the geraniums, jumped down onto the floor and began rubbing itself against the table legs with small expectant cries. "You've got to wait Tibby," Kirstie told it sternly. Surreptitiously Iain threw it a morsel of lamb.

The hot, covered dishes circulated. There were young green peas, new potatoes and baby carrots swimming in fresh butter. It was all so delicious that Susan couldn't help exclaiming. She had never, she said, eaten more perfectly cooked vegetables.

"It's not the cooking," Kirstie declaimed modestly, "but how they are grown. Iain is a keen organic gardener."

Iain raised a quizzical eyebrow. "She'll not know what you are talking about, Kirstie. She's a London-bred lass."

"Oh, no, I'm not," Susan hastened to correct him. "My home is in Sussex."

"Which is much the same thing." He gave her a provocative grin. "The whole of the south of England is a vast suburb, built-up and overcrowded. If you want to find real country and country food, grown as it ought to be grown, you've got to come to Scotland. Or better still—" the grin widened "—to Glenelg."

"And if we get onto the subject of food growing," Kirstie put in, "we'll be here for the rest of the night. My brother is a bit of a fanatic about his horticultural theories, Miss Harrowby—I'd better warn you."

"He has already told me some of his ideas," Susan said. "I found them most interesting."

"Nice, tactful girl!" Iain teased her.

Kirstie gave her a speculative glance. "I was wondering what he found to talk to you about on an eight-hour journey!"

"We found plenty," Iain declared. "And it wasn't all about gardening, by any means!"

Kirstie's shrewd glance went from one to the other. Quite clearly she was bursting with curiosity about their encounter. Susan took pity on her. "It all began," she said, "when he saved me from falling under the wheels of the train at King's Cross. It was already moving when I tried to board it."

"So I grabbed her by the shoulders and hauled her in," Iain finished it for her.

"You might have been killed," Kirstie told Susan disapprovingly. "Those big express trains pick up speed so quickly once they are moving."

"So I discovered! But I just couldn't bear to let it go without me," Susan said, and wondered if she had better go on. How much had Iain told his sister about their unexpected guest? As her hostess, Kirstie had a right to know something of the urgencies that had brought her to Edinburgh in so great a hurry that she hadn't even had time to reserve a room at a hotel.

"You must have had pressing reasons for your journey," Kirstie prompted now, as she hesitated.

"I had," Susan admitted. "I've come to try to find my young sister, Miss MacDowell." Once more Susan plunged into the painful recital. But before she had gone very far Kirstie interrupted her.

"My brother has already told me something about your trouble, Miss Harrowby. And indeed, you have my sympathy. Your sister ought to be ashamed of herself, bringing such worry and disgrace on her family. They're all the same nowadays—these so-called teenagers. No thought for anyone but themselves. A reckless, irresponsible lot."

"But Jan isn't really irresponsible," Susan said, resenting this summary judgment. "She's headstrong and impulsive, but she's no fool. And she's very kind. In the ordinary way she wouldn't dream of hurting us like this. Being in love, I suppose, does strange things to people." She met Kirstie's grim glance appealingly.

Kirstie all but snorted. "And you think a lassie of seventeen has any idea what love really means?"

"It's a possibility," Susan faltered. "She could have. . . ."

"Of course she could," Iain supported her. "Age has very little to do with it. You can meet your fate at seventeen—or seventy."

"Of all the starry-eyed nonsense!" Kirstie threw up her hands in despair. "Don't heed him, Miss Harrowby. He's an incurable romantic, for all his quiet ways. . . ."

"A wolf in sheep's clothing," Iain grinned.

But he had helped her in her defense of Jan, Susan thought gratefully.

"Elopements," he was saying now, "after all, it didn't take the present day teenager to think them up. They've been going on since the beginning of time. What about fourteen-year-old Juliet and her Romeo, or fair Ellen who rode off with young Lochinvar . . . and the bride who ran from her bridegroom at the altar into the arms of Jock of Hazledean?"

"A lot of poetic rubbish," Kirstie snapped, "putting ideas into young peoples' heads. Running away to be married against your parents' wishes is a selfish, reckless act."

"And a pretty brave one," Iain added quietly.

Kirstie glared at him. "What has come over you this evening, Iain MacDowell? It's a good thing it is Miss Harrowby and not you who has to deal with this runaway couple!" She turned to Susan, "What are you going to do, if you find them?"

"Persuade my sister to come home," Susan said. "Or at least have a good try at it."

"She's under age," Kirstie pointed out. "There are laws for dealing with her kind. . . . You'll get her home all right if you go the right way about it. Our Uncle Hamish will advise you. Iain tells me he is taking you to the office in the morning."

"It's very kind of him," Susan said in a small, crushed voice. The thought of subjecting Jan to legal pressure made her feel a little sick. She glanced across the table as if for support, and Iain did not fail her.

"Hamish is a wise old bird . . . and very human," he said. "Don't worry about it any more tonight, if you can help it . . . and don't cross your bridges before you come to them." He pushed the cheese dish toward her. "Have some of this cream cheese—Kirstie's special. I recommend it."

Tacitly, Jan and her misdemeanors were dropped and when the meal was over Iain went off to see about his dungle-dozer. Susan insisted upon helping Kirstie do the dishes. She worked swiftly and methodically, keeping up a friendly flow of chatter, thawing visibly over the shared task. "It's not the first time you have lent a hand in the kitchen," she remarked approvingly, as Susan sorted knives and forks and put them away in the correct drawers.

Like her brother she seemed to enjoy talking about Glenelg. When the electricity was installed, she confided, they might take in a few paying guests. There was room and enough to spare. "Tourists driving through to the Highlands might be tempted to break their journey here and see something of the countryside," she said. "Though it's not as dramatic as the mountains of the North, it has its own charm."

Susan, seizing the opportunity, suggested she might be the first paying guest. Kirstie silenced her indignantly. "You have come to this house as our guest," she declared, "and there can be no talk of payment. In Bencramond we often took in a benighted climber or traveler and thought nothing of it. Hospitality in the remote parts of the country is still offered as a matter of course . . . a matter of pride," she added with dignity. "So stop fretting yourself and imagining you are putting us out. Indeed," she went on with an unexpected touch of graciousness, "I am very glad to have you. It's a change to have someone to talk to. Iain is away so much on the farm that it gets lonesome . . . especially in the evenings."

She went into the scullery and came back with two tall, old-fashioned oil lamps. Susan watched her lighting them, the tension easing in her heart. Dusk had darkened the window behind the geraniums and the kitchen was bright with lamplight and the rosy glow of the fire. In a corner by the stove the tabby cat crouched comfortably over his plate of table scraps. It was all so cosy and homely . . . and Kirstie improved on acquaintance. Prickly on the surface, but solid at the core, Susan decided. A friend worth having—if she decided to be your friend!

They went upstairs to see to the guest room, Kirstie carrying one of the lamps. As they mounted the beautiful staircase she pointed to the candle sconces, empty on the walls, the great chandelier that hung over the well of the vast, shadowy hall. "It will be almost a pity to fit them with electric bulbs," she said. "What a sight they must have been, lighted with a hundred blazing wax tapers—the ladies in their silks and satins floating up and down these very stairs. . . ." She halted on the landing, looking down into the hall as if she could see the ghosts of those other more spacious days. "There are folk who would say Iain was mad to buy this great rambling place," she went on presently, "but we love its space and—its dignity. It will make a wonderful home for him one of these days . . . a bonny place to bring up a family. If . . ." she broke off to give Susan a searching glance, "he marries the right sort of girl. There are some born to be homemakers, and others who are home wreckers from the start."

Susan, for some reason embarrassed at the turn of the conversation, murmured that she was sure he would choose wisely.

"I hope you are right," Kirstie returned dryly. "But you heard him at supper. There's a touch of the dreamer in his makeup that scares me at times. Like as not, when the time comes, he'll pick on some helpless lassie with a pretty face and nothing behind it, just because she appeals to his overgrown bump of chivalry."

Not knowing what to say to this sisterly outburst, Susan kept silent.

In a vast dim bedroom that smelled of faded rose leaves they made up a huge four-poster bed. "You'll find the mattress well aired," Kirstie promised. "I had it hanging out in the sun only yesterday." From a gleaming mahogany tallboy she produced clean towels. "The water is hot, if you would like a bath. We go to bed early," she added, and Susan was only too glad to take the hint. She would have her bath straightaway, she said.

The mattress that had hung out in the sun was made of feathers, she discovered a little later, when she sank into its enveloping folds. Easing her travel weary bones into it she felt as if she were floating on a lavender-scented cloud. She had meant to lie awake a little while, sort out the long day's impressions . . . think of Jan, but before she knew where she was she was asleep.

WHEN SHE WOKE it was daylight, and the memory of Jan was a sharp stab of anguish awaiting her. Kirstie came in at half-past six with a cup of tea. "We have breakfast at half-past seven," she announced without apology. "Iain has to be away to the town with his vegetables before eight—he has regular customers for them at all the big greengroceries. Did you sleep well?" she asked.

"Like a top," Susan assured her. "This is a most seductively comfortable bed."

"We brought it with us from Bencramond," Kirstie said. "A real old family bed—generations of the MacDowells have slept in it, been born in it . . . died in it." A disconcerting thought! But why should it be, Susan reflected as she drank her heartening tea. Life beginning, flowering, quietly ending . . . in the peaceful continuity of family life. As she dressed she looked at the beautiful old bed with new interest. It seemed to have developed a personality now . . . an air of wisdom and permanency that was comforting, and it somehow made it easier to think of Jan. In the years to come, Susan thought, she would look back at this strange journey, seeing it in perspective—so small a part in the Harrowby history. If only good could come out of it for all of them in the end. Here in this tranquil room she had an odd premonition that it would indeed be so, and her heart was curiously light as she went down to breakfast.

It was a hurried meal, for Iain was already out in the stable yard, loading up his station wagon. As she drove away with him, Susan turned to look back at the gracious white house with its dark sweep of woodlands rising behind it. It seemed all at once intolerably sad to her that she might never see it again. Kirstie, to be sure, had hospitably urged her to return tonight if she was still without a place to stay. There was a bus from the city, she explained, that passed through the nearby village of Elgin-bridge. But it was all quite unreal to Susan. She must remain in Edinburgh now until she had either found Jan, or given up the search as hopeless.

As though reading her thoughts, Iain said, "I've been pondering how you could best set about looking for your sister today. Unless Uncle Hamish has anything more concrete to suggest you might spend an hour or two at the National Gallery. As your sister and her fiancé are both painters they'll be bound to visit the Festival Art Exhibition there. It's the big building like a Greek temple . . . not far from the station. You can't miss it."

"I could certainly try it," Susan agreed without much enthusiasm, and for the rest of the journey they spoke hardly at all, Iain seeming withdrawn and aloof, busy with his own thoughts. Already their roads were diverging, their brief contact coming to an end. Ridiculous to feel a twinge about it, Susan told herself firmly. For all his kindness and the odd sense of harmony between them, the man at her side was a stranger. Presently, when he left her in his uncle's office, he would walk out of her life forever. And that, most definitely, was that!

They were running into the suburbs now, and soon Iain was stopping at his various ports of call. When the last of his wares were delivered he turned the car into a wide leafy square. "Uncle Hamish's office is right here," he said, indicating one of the tall gray stone houses. "But they don't open until nine-thirty, and I doubt if old Hamish will show up much before ten. Let's fill in the time having a cup of coffee. I'll just find a place to park the car."

He took her arm as they walked toward Princes Street, guiding her through the crowd of shoppers and festival visitors. Although it was early the pavements were already congested.

"We could go to the Festival Club," he suggested. "I joined it this season with the other members of our musical society. Makes a handy rendezvous, and they do you very well." He turned to give her his quick, warm smile. "It's comfortable and quiet . . . we can talk there in peace."

Her heart gave a small involuntary leap. "Sounds good!" she said, and it was just at that moment that the bearded man in a corduroy jacket brushed against her accidentally, and stopped to apologize. She looked up into his face with a gasp of recognition—Tony Brampton! And it was Jan at his side, her dark eyes blazing with fear and defiance as they met Susan's startled gaze.

CHAPTER FIVE

FOR AN INSTANT the two girls stood transfixed, the men halting at their sides, briefly puzzled. But almost at once it was clear what had happened. Princes Street, like Piccadilly Circus, was famed for its chance encounters—especially during festival weeks. There was hardly a visitor who didn't walk its length two or three times daily, drawn by the gardens, the castle, the elegant shops, or more simply by the fact that you couldn't go from one point of interest in the city to another without traversing this main and beautiful boulevard. So that it wasn't really so extraordinary that they should all have converged on the same spot at the same moment of this fine August morning, though to Susan and Jan the coincidence seemed overwhelming.

It was Jan who managed to speak at last. "You've followed us!" she croaked in a voice not in the least like her own. "I warned you not to. Oh, Susan, you shouldn't have come!" The last words rose in a hysterical wail that attracted the attention of one or two interested passersby.

"Good heavens, your sister!" Tony Brampton could be heard to murmur—in impatience, rather than alarm. "Really, Miss Harrowby . . ." he began defensively.

Ignoring him, Susan put her hands on Jan's shoulders and dropped a quick kiss on her cheek. "Darling, it is so wonderful to see you! We've been so worried about you!

"And Tony," she added ambiguously. She turned to

him with a flustered, "I don't think we've met before, have we, Mr. Brampton? How do you do?" The conventional greeting struck her as absurd. Tony answered it with a sardonic little bow. After that they all stood staring at one another; nobody seemed to know what to do next.

There was a moment of sheer blankness. Then Iain, who had been hovering in the background, said a little awkwardly, "Well, I'd better be pushing along, Susan. You'll not be needing to call on my uncle now. . . ."

She swung around to him, her eyes wide and dark with appeal. "Please don't go, Iain!" He mustn't leave her, not yet. Instinctively she clung to his strength and his good sense. If there had been only Jan to cope with . . . but there was Tony, large, grim and bearded, looking down at her as if she were some kind of insect. An arrogant and determined man, far more than a match for her powers of argument, she suspected. She laid a pleading hand on Iain's arm. "Let me introduce you," she begged. "Jan . . . Mr. Brampton . . . this is Iain MacDowell." Hurriedly she offered the little formula, adding almost in the same breath, "We were just on our way to the Festival Club for a cup of coffee. Won't you join us?" An invitation it was hardly her place to tender.

But mercifully Iain backed her up—tacitly answering her unspoken call for help. "Yes, do come along, by all means—jolly good idea." He smiled at Tony, inclined his head slightly to Jan. "It's just around the corner on George Street."

Jan and Tony exchanged glances. As their eyes met Jan's defiant face softened, became submissive, adoring—the look of a girl head over heels in love. Whatever he says, she'll do, Susan thought with an odd sharp pang. She saw Tony's answering look confident, possessive . . . yet reassuringly tender. He said, "We'd better accept that cup of coffee, my dear. Your sister has come a long way to offer it to us. And a little chat may clear the air."

"It won't," Jan declared doggedly. "However . . . ." She hunched her slim shoulders in an expressive shrug.

Somehow they were on their way then: Jan and Susan walking together, the men tactfully dropping behind a pace or two. As they made their way through the crowd Susan took Jan's arm. She could hardly believe her search was so simply over; drawing Jan close to her she felt quite light-headed with relief.

"You needn't clutch onto me as if I were a prisoner," Jan muttered ungraciously. "I'm not going to bolt! But if you imagine you are going to talk me into going home with you you're crazy!"

Susan fought back a wave of rising anger. She'd got to be patient . . . remember Jan was at bay, more than a little scared, perhaps, in spite of her jaunty air. She said gently, "Jan dear, I don't think you quite realize what we've all been through at home during the last few days. Mother and dad are simply shot to pieces—"

"It's their own fault," Jan broke in. "If they had been more reasonable about Tony and me we wouldn't have had to run away. You weren't there when the crisis came . . . you've no idea how shattering it all was. They were simply horrible to poor Tony." Her voice faltered ominously. "I'd never have thought they could be so cruel!"

"They don't mean to be cruel," Susan said quickly, placatingly. "It's just that they are worried to death about you. You're so young, Jan, so inexperienced. After all, you've known Tony so short a time. They are terrified you may ruin your life."

"So they've decided to make sure and ruin it for me,"

Jan retorted. "Or at least they will if I let them. Why can't they trust me a little? I know Tony far better than they do. I may be young, but I'm no fool." She jerked her arm free impatiently. "Honestly, Susan, I'm amazed at you, coming all this way to badger me . . . spy on me. I thought you'd have been on my side."

"I am on your side . . . that's why I'm here."

"Oh, for Pete's sake don't try to be subtle!" Jan snapped. "I know exactly why you're here. In fact I could probably repeat word for word the hectic family confab there was when my letter arrived yesterday—with an Edinburgh postmark. I ought not to have sent it."

"It would have been horribly unkind *not* to," Susan declared with a touch of heat.

Jan made a weary little gesture. "Oh, well, don't let us argue about it. You've tracked me down, and that's that. But I warn you you're wasting your time." They walked on in troubled silence, and presently Jan said with a rather desperate attempt at lightness, "By the way, just where did you pick up the good-looking Scotsman you've got in tow? You seem to be on pretty familiar terms with him."

Poor Jan, trying so hard to seem at ease, but inwardly floundering between guilt and defiance. Susan was not for a moment deceived, sensing in her very bravado her young bewilderment, her unhappiness at the pain she was giving her family. They had always been so united—and Jan adored her father. Surely these lifelong ties that bound her would prove stronger in the end than the pull of a teenage romance—the hero worship of a student for a master. At a first glance, Tony Brampton had seemed to Susan formidable rather than attractive, the domineering type. Not at all the sort of husband to handle the high-spirited Jan successfully. As she would no doubt discover, tragically, when it was too late.

I've got to make her realize all this. . . . Please, God help me! Susan prayed inwardly, wordlessly.

Briefly she recounted her meeting with Iain MacDowell on the train the day before, her fruitless attempt to find accommodation when they arrived in Edinburgh, and how Iain had insisted upon taking her home to his sister. "She's nice," Susan ended it a little lamely. "They're both nice."

"He looks a pet," Jan agreed, and for the first time sounded warm and natural . . . wholly herself.

But they had reached the club now. Iain led the way up a flight of steps into an impressive foyer filled with flowers. There were wide doors leading to a reading room, a writing room, a restaurant and a snack bar. It was all very well-ordered, even luxurious.

"We'll go into the lounge," Iain elected. In the large, sunny room that they had, at this hour, practically to themselves, they settled in comfortable armchairs ranged around a low glass-topped table. A waitress appeared at once to take their order.

Tony said, "All very well run, isn't it? How does one join this club?"

"Oh, it's perfectly simple," Iain assured him. "As festival visitors you can apply for daily or weekly membership, or there is a seasonal membership at a minimum charge. If you want to entertain friends you can buy guest tickets—quite reasonably. I always keep a book or two of these tickets by me. . . ." They talked on in a desultory way about the club and its amenities. Then Jan launched into a glowing account of a festival symphony concert they had attended the night before.

This is getting us nowhere, Susan thought desperately. Leaning back in her chair she waited for an opportunity to bring the conversation back to more relevant matters, her glance going nervously from one face to another. Jan, wearing a vivid coral jersey suit, looked breathtakingly lovely. There was a new glow to her beauty, an odd maturity in her bearing that made her seem much more than her seventeen years—a woman desired, and desiring. Iain, Susan noticed, couldn't take his eyes off her. Neither could Tony . . . which was understandable. Covertly Susan studied him—a large, ruggedly built man in an aggressively casual polo-necked sweater and corduroy jacket. His thick reddish brown hair was a little too long, his small pointed beard consciously "arty." It hid too much of his face, Susan decided; you couldn't judge a person's character nearly so well when the mouth and chin were concealed. But his eyes were reassuring, wide and candid and very blue, giving him an almost ingenuous air—the eyes of a visionary. You couldn't imagine their owner doing anything underhanded or dishonest. And yet hadn't he been both, a little, in his handling of his affairs with Jan?

"They ended with a gorgeous Bartok concerto," she was saying. "The violin solo was out of this world. It was the Scottish National Orchestra. . . ." She turned to Iain. "You ought to be very proud of it, Mr. MacDowell."

"I am," Iain agreed with a nod. "If you want to hear it again it will be giving another performance at the Usher Hall on Saturday—Mozart and Rossini."

"We'll certainly try to get tickets," Tony said enthusiastically.

"If you are still in Edinburgh!" Susan put in quietly.

There was an instant's electrical silence, and then Jan said sharply, "Where else would we be?"

Susan took a deep breath. "I don't know. That's what I hoped we would talk about."

Tony produced a cigarette case from his pocket and flicking it open, offered it to Susan, then to Jan. "By all means," he said evenly, "let us discuss our plans."

Iain moved restlessly in his chair. "If you'd rather I left you . . ." he began diffidently.

Susan flung him an imploring glance, but it was Jan, surprisingly, who urged him to stay. "You can listen to all the pros and cons, if we've got to have pros and cons . . . and give the casting vote." She smiled at him impishly as he leaned over to light the cigarette that dangled from her red lips. Susan saw an odd little quiver pass over his lean face as he watched her dark head bend over the offered flame. She looked up at him, inhaling expertly. "Has Susan told you about us?" she demanded bluntly.

"Yes," Susan answered for him. "I have. I was so bursting with worry in the train yesterday I simply had to confide in somebody."

"So you picked on Mr. MacDowell," Jan teased. "Just like that!"

"No," Iain said a trifle stiffly. "Not just like that . . . if you mean there were no preliminaries. I had to do quite a spot of prompting. We shared a meal in the restaurant car. I could see your sister was deeply troubled. I urged her to talk because I thought it might ease her mind a bit. Believe me, Miss Harrowby, I wasn't simply being idly curious."

Jan had the grace to look ashamed.

"It was just . . ." Susan halted apologetically, "that I felt so lost. It seemed so crazy to be hurrying off to Edinburgh with no idea where to begin looking for you. . . ."

"It *was* crazy," Tony agreed dryly. "But now that you've found us in this extraordinarily simple fashion, what do you propose to do about it?"

"Try to persuade Jan to come home with me," Susan returned a little breathlessly.

"Give me one good reason why I should?" Jan demanded.

"Well . . ." Susan floundered for a moment, "there's

your love for mother and dad . . . your duty to them. You are still a child in their eyes, a very dear child, and the way they see it you are acting in a way that could ruin your whole life.''

"Thanks!" Tony broke in with a hard little laugh.

Susan swung around on him. "Jan is only seventeen. Supposing you were in our parents' place . . . supposing she were *your* daughter?"

"Meaning," said Tony, "she is young enough to be?"

"Well . . . almost," Susan faltered.

"That's nonsense," Jan put in sharply. "Tony is barely thirty. Lots of girls marry men older than themselves."

"And anyway," Tony went on with it, "age is relative. Jan is grown-up for her age, amazingly so in many ways. She doesn't think like a seventeen-year-old . . . she doesn't paint like a seventeen-year-old—"

"And I don't fall in love like a seventeen-year-old," Jan added softly. She put her hand out to Tony and he took it and held it fast. For a long moment they gazed at one another, lost to their surroundings. Susan and Iain exchanged a baffled glance. Leaning toward her he said in an undertone, "I'm not doing very much to help you, I'm afraid!"

"Just having you here is a help," Susan told him fervently.

"They're conspiring against us, Tony," Jan laughed. She turned to Iain, her dark head tilted provocatively. "I'm surprised at you, Mr. MacDowell. I was hoping you'd be on our side."

Iain stiffened a little and his thin face went rather stern . . . as if Jan's flippancy jarred him, Susan thought.

"It's hardly my place to take sides in your personal affairs, Miss Harrowby,'' he said coolly. "And I'm no great authority on love . . . but it seems a pity to me that it should be allowed to split any family apart.''

Jan gave a childish pout. "If we are being split apart it is entirely due to my parents' attitude. I'd no idea they could be so—prehistoric. They make not the slightest effort to understand how it really is between Tony and me.''

"Because they are incapable of understanding," Tony declared. "Their minds are rigidly conventional . . . and I don't happen to conform to type—therefore, I'm suspect. To begin with I'm a painter; my living is precarious. I'm not offering Jan lifelong security and a fat insurance policy to take care of her if I should come to an untimely end. I'm offering her instead a ramshackle studio home in Paris where she can share with me something I value much more highly than security—that is the adventure of painting, an endless road that we can take together, a hard way, but rewarding . . . the daily struggle to discover and express certain aspects of truth. What better foundation could there be for any marriage?" His blue eyes blazed. "A community of interests . . . the pursuit of a vision forever elusive, forever fresh." He looked straight at Susan. "Do you think some stockbroker chappie commuting from Moorings to the city could offer your sister anything half as vital, or as likely to make for the best sort of happiness?''

"Darling!" Jan breathed, quite overcome by this outburst of eloquence.

Susan said thoughtfully, "You put it very persuasively, Tony, and I do, up to a point, agree. Being interested in the same things must be a good foundation for any marriage. But you could surely have taken a little more trouble to win my parents around to your point of view? You weren't very tactful from what I can gather. If you'd waited a little longer—"

"Tact!" Tony spat the word out in scorn. "Compromise . . . waiting, letting the months and maybe the years drift by, with me in Paris and Jan plodding on at that deadly little school in Oakford, which incidentally was well on the way to ruining her considerable talent." He threw out his arms in passionate gesticulation. "Jan isn't just any run-of-the-mill little art student, Miss Harrowby. She has vision, originality, the individual approach that in any creative work is well on the way to genius."

"Would you have felt the same way about her if you hadn't happened to fall in love with her?" Susan asked levelly.

Tony thrust impatient hands through his thick hair. "Of all the Philistine questions! Of course I would. I'd have moved heaven and earth to rescue her from Oakford. The moment I saw her work I knew she ought to be spending her formative years in Paris . . . in Rome. And now that she can, as my wife, live with me in these places I don't intend to let anything hinder her. There's no question of us hanging around for two or three years while your father makes up his mind to accept the inevitable. It is Jan's career that is at stake . . . her whole life, her happiness . . . her soul, if you like. . . ."

There was complete silence for a moment, then Iain said with a little laugh. "Well, that seems to have carried us about as far as we can go. Defense rests. Glad I'm not the prosecuting counsel!" He beckoned to a passing waitress to bring the bill.

Susan watched him pay it, with a heavy heart. There might not be any easy answers to Tony's passionate arguments, but there were still many things to be considered. Her father's dogged determination to stop the marriage at any cost . . . his frightening hint at legal proceedings. . . .

They all stood up. In a few moments Iain would be leaving them . . . hurrying back to his all-absorbing life at Glenelg. In a day or two he would have forgotten the Harrowbys and their family squabble. *And we've settled really nothing,* Susan thought bleakly. She had a completely illogical feeling that if she could only hold on to Iain a little longer she might see more clearly what she ought to do. What did he think of Tony, for instance? It would be helpful to have his opinion. She wondered if she could snatch a private word with him before he vanished. But he was walking apart from her as they drifted out into the hot sunshine, asking Jan and Tony if they were comfortably fixed at their hotel.

"We're at the Balrogie Hotel in Montrose Crescent," Jan told him. "It is small, but quite good. My room is a big double one, so Susan could share it with me tonight." She linked her arm affectionately through her sister's. "Do stay, Sue. You can't go rushing back to Moorings after coming all this way without one glimpse of the festival. We're going to the ballet tonight. You could phone home and let the folks know you are with us," she urged. "Come to that, we could all three have a word with them. After six, when the cheap rates are available. You could plead for us Sue . . . help us to get some sense into their dear old heads."

"What a hope!" Tony broke in rather bitterly. "This isn't the sort of thing you can put right over the phone."

"It certainly isn't!" Susan agreed. Her color ebbed a little as she turned to Jan and her mouth went tight and grim.

"You just don't realize the mood dad is in, Jan. He says he will go to any lengths to stop your marriage to Tony, and I know he means it." She was putting it too bluntly, but suddenly it seemed to her that she must make a stand. Jan, poor child, seemed to think Tony's eloquent arguments had swept all difficulties away . . . that a lighthearted conversation tonight on the phone would convince her parents they had been wrong in opposing her, and that, anyway, she was with her lover for keeps.

She turned startled brown eyes on her sister. "How do you mean 'go to any lengths': what can he do?"

"You're under age, Jan. It gives dad certain rights over you—legal rights. There are steps he can take to bring you home . . . even against your will."

It was out now—the ultimatum she had hoped she wouldn't be forced to deliver. She saw Tony halt and swing around to face her. For a moment they all just stood there, stock-still. It was as if she had dropped a bomb in their midst, Susan thought, and in a mesmerized way they now waited for it to go off. Tony's cheeks, above the beard, went an odd mottled color. He said with forced quietness, "That settles it. Now we really do know where we are!" He took Jan's hand and drew her to his side. She looked up at him drowningly, waiting for his lead. She had gone very white and her lips trembled.

He said, "Sorry, Susan, but there'll be no ballet tonight, no sharing of rooms at the Balrogie Hotel. This is where our roads diverge." He nodded his massive head in careless farewell. "Goodbye, been nice seeing you . . . and MacDowell, and thanks a lot for the coffee." Resolutely he turned on his heel. "Come along, poppet." He tucked Jan's hand through his arm and began marching her away. She had to run a little to keep up with his long impatient strides, looking back over her shoulder to call to Susan distractedly, "It's all right . . . don't look so tragic. I'll . . . write . . . sometime. Let you know how things go. . . ."

In another moment they would turn the corner into crowded Princes Street and be lost to sight. Conscious only of panic, Susan darted after them. "Jan!" she called desperately. "Where are you going?" She clutched at Tony's jacket sleeve. Gently he shook her off. His blue eyes were not unkindly, looking down at her.

"It's no use, Susan. Be a good girl and buzz off. You've said your piece and we've listened to you, and now there is only one thing left for us to do . . . clear out of Edinburgh . . . to a place where you won't so easily find us. Your father's attitude . . . and his threats are no surprise to me. I'm not without plans."

"Oh, Susan, darling, you're making it so hard for us!" There were tears in Jan's eyes as she flung her arms around her sister's neck. "Goodbye. Just go home and stop worrying. I'll be all right. Really!"

"Come on, Jan, no use prolonging the agony." Impatiently Tony turned aside, so certain that Jan would follow him that he didn't bother to look around to make sure she was close behind.

Just what happened next Susan would never be quite sure, but it seemed as if Tony, large and vital and restive, was there one moment—poised on the pavement's edge, and the next moment he had vanished. There was a shout, a grinding of brakes . . . then a sudden terrible silence in which the whole sun-filled, busy street seemed to come to a standstill. On the curb where Tony had been, Jan stood, her hands to her face in a frozen gesture, her brown eyes glazing with horror as they looked down at the motionless form in the gutter at her feet.

CHAPTER SIX

A NIGHTMARE interlude followed. After the first frozen pause things began to move at a sinister speed—as though the whole ghastly drama had been arranged beforehand. A policeman, appearing from nowhere, waved authoritative arms at the rapidly gathering crowd of onlookers, another policeman bent over the form in the gutter; in loud aggrieved tones a van driver disclaimed all responsibility for the accident. "Walked right into me near-side mudguard," he kept shouting. "I hadn't a chance of avoiding him."

This can't be happening to us! Susan thought in stunned disbelief. There was a hollow feeling inside her head, and her legs didn't seem to belong to her. She saw Iain supporting the half-fainting Jan in his arms and heard the spine chilling clamor of an ambulance's siren. But it was all very confused.

Afterward, she couldn't remember getting into the ambulance, only that somehow she found herself there, sitting on a small swivel chair that swayed disconcertingly every time they rounded a corner. Tony, wrapped in blankets on a stretcher, might have been peacefully sleeping save for the deathly pallor of his face, and the ugly gash above one temple from which a bright scarlet thread trickled. A uniformed nurse was counting his pulse rate. Jan, huddled at his side, watched her breathlessly. "If he dies, I shall die, too!" she whispered through dry lips.

Susan leaned over and took one of her cold hands. "He's not going to die, darling," she offered helplessly.

"Of course he's not," the nurse declared, just a shade too heartily. "His pulse rate is quite good . . . considering. But we ought to do something about that bleeding." She busied herself with bandages and pads and was fixing the last pin in place when they swung through the hospital gates. Getting out of the ambulance, Susan looked around for Iain, who had stayed behind at the scene of the accident to answer the inevitable official questions. He would follow on in his car, he had promised—to her intense relief. It seemed so natural to depend on him at this terrible moment, so difficult to remember they had no real claim on him.

They went through swinging doors into a wide, green-painted corridor. Tony on his stretcher was being whisked away through another door marked Casualty. "If you will wait here we will let you have the doctor's report as soon as possible," the ambulance nurse told them.

They sat down on a plain wooden bench. The corridor was warm and empty and silent. Sunlight from high windows filtered down on the endless vista of polished floor. After the fever and terror of the last half hour it was like being dropped into a sea-colored vacuum. Susan had an almost irresistible desire to close her eyes and go to sleep. Shock, she thought dully. Odd what a merciful thing it could be . . . like an anaesthetic, cutting one off from reality that had suddenly become too grim to bear. But she mustn't give in to it; there was Jan to think of, rigid at her side as a block of marble, only her dark eyes blazingly alive, fixed on the mottled glass door through which Tony had vanished. Susan swallowed a lump in her throat. It was dreadful to see her like this, all her happy animation gone. In a matter of moments she had been changed from a girl radiantly in love to this ashen-faced automaton.

The mottled glass door opened and a nurse appeared, a sheaf of papers in her hand. Could they give her the patient's particulars, she asked—age, profession, home address, next of kin.

Jan, who had started up hopefully at the sight of her, sank into apathy again. "Mr. Brampton has no family . . . no next of kin," she said. "There's only me. . . ."

"Are you a relative?" the nurse inquired.

"We are close friends," Susan put in quickly. She gave Jan a warning glance. This was no time to go into details about runaway marriages. If they were to avoid the unpleasant publicity their father so much dreaded they would have to be very careful what they said to the hospital authorities. An elopement that had ended in a street accident . . . Susan could well imagine the sensational newspaper headlines if the story got out. "Mr. Brampton is an artist by profession," she told the nurse. "His home is in Paris."

The nurse looked baffled. "But there ought to be someone with whom we could get in touch if . . . if it becomes necessary."

If Tony were to die, she too obviously meant. Jan clenched her hands on her lap. "You can get in touch with me," she said.

"At Glenelg House, Elginbridge," Iain's voice chimed in behind them. Susan turned to him with a lifting heart. Engrossed with the nurse and her difficult questions, she hadn't noticed him come in. But now he was here everything seemed much easier. The very sight of him, tall and strong and imperturbable, was enough to rob the situation of half its menace.

"Telephone: Elginbridge thirty-four," he was saying to the nurse. "Ask for Miss Harrowby, Miss Jan Harrowby."

The nurse thanked him and went away.

Iain sat down on the bench beside Jan. She looked up at him with a stupefied air. "But you gave her the wrong address . . . I'm staying at the Balrogie Hotel. . . ."

He slid a protective arm along the back of the bench behind her. "From now on you're staying at Glenelg." He smiled down at the tense uplifted face in gentle compassion. "I phoned Kirstie, my sister, on the way to the hospital and told her . . . we'd run into a spot of trouble. She insists I'm to bring you and Susan home with me when we're through with the formalities here."

Susan heard him with mixed feelings, in which relief and an indefinable sense of reprieve were uppermost. But it was all wrong, they couldn't keep accepting help from the kindly MacDowells indefinitely. "Iain, we can't . . ." she began protestingly.

He held up a silencing hand. "No arguments, now! It's all settled. We can't have you and Jan worrying this out alone in some cold-hearted hotel. At least come to us until you know how things are shaping for Brampton. He may be all right in a day or two."

Jan scanned his face hungrily. "You're just saying that to kid me along!"

"No, I'm not, my dear." He patted her arm reassuringly. "It's just that I believe in looking on the bright side of things. It never does any harm."

Nor any good, Jan's sagging shoulders seemed to say as she turned away from him to resume her gimlet-eyed watch on the mottled glass door. When it opened to reveal an authoritative advancing nurse, Susan heard her draw in a quick, rasping breath. The nurse glanced at them inquiringly. "Mr. Brampton's friends?" she asked. They all stood up.

The nurse said gently, "Mr. Brampton's injuries are pretty extensive I'm afraid. We won't be able to make a complete diagnosis until he has been given an X-ray examination. But there seems to be some concussion as a result of the head wound, as well as a broken shoulder and three damaged ribs. Meanwhile, it is unlikely that he will regain consciousness for several hours . . . or even days . . . or . . . ." She left the sentence ominously unfinished, and as if to obliterate the gloomy implication smiled hearteningly at the little group. "So there isn't much point in your waiting any longer just now, is there? We will get in touch with you at once if there is any change in the patient's condition." She was ushering them toward the door as she spoke. "Visiting hours," she said, "are from seven to eight each evening, and on Wednesday and Sunday afternoons. If you would like to come in tomorrow—" she was looking compassionately at Jan "—you may be able to see Mr. Brampton for a few minutes."

"Can't I see him now before I leave?" Jan begged in a thread of a voice.

The nurse shook her head. "I'm afraid not, my dear. And it wouldn't be any use. He wouldn't know you." She turned to Susan in kindly concern. "This child looks to me as if she is suffering from quite a degree of shock. You'd better get her home and put her to bed."

They went out into the late August sunshine. It seemed incredible to find the world going on as usual—women with shopping baskets hurrying along the pavements, errand boys whistling on bicycles, buses clattering down the long hill to the city's center. Somewhere a clock chimed eleven. An hour ago they had all been sitting in the Festival Club drinking coffee . . . arguing about a wedding that now seemed too remote a contingency to be worth a thought. Susan's eyes filled with tears. How quickly and tragically the whole situation had altered!

The station wagon was parked outside the hospital gates. They got into it in silence. There was room for both girls in front with Iain. He took them first to the Balrogie Hotel. It was Susan who went in to collect Jan and Tony's luggage and settle the bill—from the almost untouched wad of notes her father had given her before she left home. Jan, slumped in her seat, seemed hardly aware of what was going on around her.

Susan got back into the car and put a firm young arm around her, meeting Iain's anxious glance over the bowed dark head. "Just what is shock supposed to do to people?" he asked in a worried undertone.

"Makes them feel deadly sick for one thing!" came the muffled reply—from Jan, who spoke through teeth that chattered. "Can you get me to . . . wherever it is we're going . . . soon?"

"I'll be as quick as I can," Iain promised, and thereafter concentrated on his driving—ignoring speed limits, eating up the miles.

Kirstie was out on the front porch waiting for them, all kindliness and concern. So this was the runaway bride! But her disapproval of Jan's lack of consideration for her parents seemed to have vanished. There was nothing but sympathy on her rugged face as she watched the pitifully sagging figure being helped up the steps. "Take her straight up and put her to bed," she advised Susan. "If you don't mind having her in with you . . . just for to-night. . . ."

"No, of course I don't. That four-poster bed is big enough for three. . . ."

"I'll bring you a hot-water bottle in a moment." Kirstie dived for the kitchen. It was no moment to begin arguing about the terms on which they were returning to Glenelg, but later, Susan determined, she'd have it out with the MacDowells; insist that they pay their way.

Jan spoke not a word as Susan helped her to undress. If only she would weep! There was something frightening about her glassy-eyed silence.

Kirstie appeared with the hot-water bottle. Iain had left the luggage outside the bedroom door; she helped Susan to carry it in before she left them—a knapsack, obviously Tony's, and two suitcases filled with the smart new clothes Jan had bought for her honeymoon. Groping in one of them Susan fished out a brand-new, rose chiffon nightie—there seemed to be nothing more practical at hand. Jan slipped it over her head with a perceptible shudder.

"I bought this for my wedding night," she said. Suddenly her face convulsed. "It was all your fault, Susan!" she cried. "If you hadn't been nagging at Tony, saying father was going to take legal action, he wouldn't have rushed away and stepped under that van."

"Jan!" Susan was too taken aback by this unexpected attack to say anything more. And there was no defense she could offer.

Jan flung herself down on the bed and buried her face in the pillows. Drawing the covers up over her, Susan crept away. She felt sick and shaken by the things Jan had said. And in a way they were true. If Tony died she would be to blame.

In the kitchen she found Kirstie heating chicken broth over the stove. "A hot drink and a couple of aspirins might help Jan get to sleep,'' she said. She took a covered soup bowl from the dresser. Susan watched her dully. This would be as good a moment as any to settle the matter of their return to Glenelg.

"It was sweet of you to tell Iain to bring us home with him," she began uncertainly. "But you've got to have us as paying guests this time, Kirstie, please!"

Kirstie glanced at her in kindly exasperation. "Dearie! Dearie! Can't you leave it for now? Iain is the master in this house, and I know well what his wishes would be."

"Then I'll talk to Iain," Susan persisted.

Kirstie shook her head. "I wouldn't do that, my dear. He's no easy man to argue with. Just leave it for a wee while and stop worrying. If it would make you any happier you can do a few little things to help now and then. Pick some of the fruit maybe . . . there's a garden full of it, waiting to be bottled and jammed and I can't seem to get around to it. If I don't get on to it soon the birds will have the lot."

"I'll start picking this afternoon," Susan promised. She took the bowl of soup and went upstairs. Jan glanced up uneasily as she entered the bedroom. Lying against the heaped pillows in her rose-colored nightgown she looked very young and wan and appealing. Her dark eyes, wide and tearless, held a fixed desolation that pierced Susan's heart.

"I ought not to have said that to you about nagging Tony," she murmured contritely. "I didn't really mean it."

Susan melted instantly, her resentment vanishing. "I know you didn't, darling. But I'm afraid it was true."

Jan shook her head. "If it was anyone's fault, it was the parents'. They ought to have left us alone, but they had to send you tearing after us." Her pale little face hardened. "They'll be delighted when they hear of Tony's accident!"

"No they won't, Jan. That's a cruel thing to say. They'll be terribly shocked . . . and very sorry for you." Once more Susan had to swallow her resentment. Jan needed comfort today, not scolding. "Who knows," Susan hazarded wildly, "this may make all the difference to their attitude. By the time Tony recovers they may well have withdrawn their opposition to the wedding."

"*If* he recovers!" Jan said stonily.

Susan put the soup down on the bedside table. "Kirstie sent you this hot drink and some aspirins to help you to get to sleep."

"Sleep!" Jan echoed bitterly. "I don't feel as if I shall ever sleep again." But she swallowed the aspirins obediently and sipped at the hot broth. "They're kind . . . your MacDowell's," she murmured absently. "It was clever of you to find them. Iain is an absolute pet!" Her voice brightened a little. "I don't know what I'd have done without him this morning. I . . . think I'd have died!" She gazed forlornly into space reliving the moments of horror.

"Try not to think about it, darling," Susan advised.

Jan drew in a shuddering breath. "How can I help thinking about it?" She gave Susan a long bleak look. "I felt so awful at the hospital when you said we were just close friends of Tony's. Why didn't you want me to tell them I was his fiancée . . . practically his wife?"

Susan sat down on the side of the bed. "Look, Jan, you don't want a lot of stupid publicity over this, do you? Newspapers always make such a fuss over lovers who elope to Scotland, and once they realize Tony is Anthony Brampton, A.R.A., you can imagine the sensation it would be. I can just see the headlines: 'Famous painter eloping with seventeen-year-old art student seriously injured in Edinburgh street accident!' ''

Jan stared at her in fascinated horror. "Gosh, I hadn't thought of that!"

"It would be the last straw to poor mother and dad to have your name bandied about all over the place," Susan went on. "You know what a gossipy little place Moorings is . . . how the villagers would talk. . . .''

Jan nodded. "I was so happy I didn't care what people might say about my running away with Tony. But now . . .'' her voice broke ominously, "now that it has turned into such a ghastly mess I'd hate to think of them . . . gloating. . . .''

"They wouldn't exactly gloat," Susan defended their not unkindly neighbors.

"Sandra Trent would," Jan said. "She's the daughter of those rich London people who bought Moorings Manor last year. I don't suppose you've met her . . . a blonde with green eyes, all glamour and sex appeal. Crazy about Tony, in fact, it was through her he came to Moorings in the first place—old man Trent had commissioned him to paint her portrait. He stayed at the manor while he was doing it, and from what he tells me he had quite a job to get away, the glamour puss having made up her mind to marry him. She was livid when she began to suspect he had taken up with me. . . .''

"So I rather gathered," Susan put in. "She was at the station the other night . . . when I was rushing home. Mother had phoned me to tell me you had vanished—"

"So you *have* met her!" The effect of this information was electrical. Jan sat up, looking almost animated. "What do you mean, you gathered she was livid about me and Tony?"

"Oh, she obviously knew who I was and insisted on giving me a lift to the house. All the way there she kept trying to pump me, asking me where you were . . . and so on. I could see she guessed there was something in the wind . . . and she had been hanging around the station, meeting trains, hoping you or Tony or both of you would turn up."

"Gosh!" Jan sighed in simple gratification. "I ran into her the morning I was making my getaway. She was in the parcels office at the station collecting a package. I'd left my cases there the night before under cover of darkness." Jan had the grace to look faintly ashamed. "We had to be careful, you see. We didn't travel up to London together, Tony and I, though we were on the same train. When Sandra asked me where I was off to, I told her I was taking some canvases up to town for a student's art show. She must have hung around then until she spotted Tony."

"She did," Susan confirmed. "She pretended he'd told her he was going to some exhibition or other and had more or less asked her to meet him on his return."

"What a fairy tale! Tony never spoke to her that morning." Jan actually laughed. "Tell me every word she said to you," she demanded eagerly.

Susan went over her encounter with Sandra again, making the most of it, spinning it out as long as she could, thankful it was proving such a diversion. Anything to take Jan's mind off the horror of the accident for a few moments. By the time she had finished some of the tension had gone out of the small face and the dark lashes had begun to droop.

"You'll sleep now," Susan said firmly, taking the empty soup cup. "I'm going downstairs now to phone the folks. They haven't a clue where I am, or what has been happening since I left home, and they'll be worried stiff.'' At the door she hesitated. "Have you any message for mother?'' she asked.

Jan's lips trembled. "Tell her . . . just tell her I love her,'' she said in a small voice. "And that I'm terribly sorry if . . . if I've made her sad.''

"I'll tell her,'' Susan said in a voice that wasn't quite under control. She could feel the tears threatening, but she managed to close the door behind her before they came. Suddenly it was all too much for her—the long strain of the last thirty-six hours, culminating in this morning's horror. And somehow Jan's pathetic message to her mother was the last straw. It was all so pitiful . . . so hopeless. Shutting herself into the bathroom Susan sobbed her heart out, and it was some time before she was able to go downstairs to make her phone call. But the weeping helped, releasing the tension, and by the time she had washed her face and repaired the ravages she felt almost brave again—able to go on.

CHAPTER SEVEN

FOR AN INTERMINABLE, anxious week Tony Brampton's condition remained unchanged. Jan, stony-faced and dry-eyed lived through the days waiting for the evening hour when she was permitted to visit him. But each time she came back to Glenelg with the same discouraging report—there was no sign of Tony regaining consciousness. Susan ached for her, but there was little she could do to help. Jan drifted around the place in a grieving trance from which she would not rouse herself until Tony woke to call her name.

Meanwhile life at Glenelg flowed smoothly. In spite of her concern for Jan, Susan enjoyed the pleasant routine. Was it heartless of her to be so happy, she wondered a little guiltily. But the days were touched with magic to which she dared not put a name. It was the charm of the old house that fascinated her, she told herself; the novelty of being in the country and working with her hands after years of being cooped up in a city office.

"When I said you could help me in the house I didn't mean you were to turn yourself into a charwoman," Kirstie protested one day as they cleaned out the drawing room together.

"But I'm loving every minute of it," Susan assured her, and paused in her dusting to admire the long elegant windows and corniced ceiling, the exquisite Adam fireplace where Kirstie knelt, as though before an altar, lovingly polishing the antique brass fire irons. By sedulously attending auction sales she was gradually acquiring, at bargain prices, the period furniture the beautiful octagonal room demanded.

"People shy off these big old houses nowadays," she remarked, rubbing away, "because of the work they entail. But I say, a home repays every bit of work you put into it. I wouldn't give a thank you for one of these modern labor-saving brick boxes that are all the fashion with lazy folk. And the joke of it is they cost more than twice the sum we paid for Glenelg." She sat back on her heels and looked around her with a sigh of satisfaction. "Maybe I'm just a sentimental old woman," she said softly, "but I like to think of Iain's children, and grandchildren, growing up in these gracious rooms. . . ." Poor Kirstie, living her life for Iain, dreaming her dreams for him. Would she really welcome it when he brought a wife home? But there was a sense of permanence in Glenelg, a putting down of roots.

In the walled kitchen garden where Susan picked fruit in the long sunny afternoons the ancient yew hedges and worn brick paths were much as they had been for three hundred years. Often Iain would leave his work to join her, on the pretext of showing her which bushes should first be stripped. Or he would take her on tours of inspection, showing her his newly made asparagus beds and compost-grown autumn strawberries, the nectarines ripening on a sheltered south wall. In the fields that sloped below the garden, lettuces and greens were cultivated on a commercial scale. In addition, root crops for livestock winter feeding had to be produced. And there were the sheep to be tended. Susan began to realize the work it all involved. A couple of day laborers came from the village to help out, but even so she sometimes wondered how it was that Iain could spare so much time talking to her, and showing her around. It was simply, she told herself, that like most men he enjoyed riding his hobby . . . having a sympathetic listener.

He came into the kitchen one golden evening to find her clamping the seals on a neat array of bottled raspberries. "You do it as though to the manner born," he teased her. "I'd no idea you were so domesticated."

"I'd no idea myself," she laughed, "having spent most of my life bashing a typewriter!"

"And you don't find it dull working in a farm kitchen instead?"

"Dull!" she echoed with a throb in her voice. "I adore it . . . find it absolutely fascinating."

"Because it's a novelty. You'd soon begin to tire of it . . . miss the bright lights of London."

"No, I wouldn't. I'd trade one of Kirstie's beautiful oil lamps for all the neon signs in Piccadilly."

He gazed at her thoughtfully, his dark hazel eyes intent. "You might find it a very different story when the beautiful oil lamps have to be lighted at three o'clock on a November afternoon. It's not much fun, I can tell you, groping through the winters here without electricity. Then the snow comes and the drifts pile up in the valley and we are cut off from the high road for a week at a time. . . ."

"Are you trying to scare me?" Susan asked lightly.

"No," he said softly, "just warning you . . . telling you the worst." The silence that followed was oddly charged. Susan's hand wasn't quite steady as she tackled the last jar. Iain watched her fumbling efforts for a moment then took the jar from her and fixed the cover himself. "Kirstie is working you too hard," he said gruffly. "Come on out for a breather . . . it will do you good."

As they walked up the wooded hill behind the house they talked of Jan, who had gone off to the hospital as usual on the late afternoon bus. "Poor kid," Iain said. "She has had a grim time of it this week, and it isn't easy to help her. She shuts you out with that stony reserve of hers."

"She has always been like that," Susan said. "Self-contained and independent—going her own wild way."

"But going it with her eyes wide open," Iain added. "Knowing what she is about."

"You mean we ought not to have interfered over her marriage to Tony?" Susan asked, troubled.

Iain pondered the question. "I suppose it was natural for your parents to get into a flap when she ran away. But perhaps they needn't have let it come to that. She's pretty sensible for her age, young Jan, able to look after herself, I would have thought. The high-spirited sort you can lead, but never drive."

"You're absolutely right there," Susan agreed, amazed at his insight.

"If I'd been in your father's place I'd have handed her over to Brampton with a sigh of relief," Iain declared with unexpected force. "As an unmarried daughter she'd be quite a handful, I imagine. Those striking good looks of hers . . . and her strong personality." He lifted the ash plant he was carrying and lashed savagely at a bunch of nettles. "As long as she's unattached she'll play havoc with hearts. . . ."

Susan felt her own heart contract—and hated herself for the swift stab of jealousy. Why shouldn't Iain say Jan was beautiful, irresistible . . . a disturber of all masculine peace of mind? It was no more than the truth. But for the first time in her life Susan resented having it pointed out to her.

They walked in silence. It was very quiet and golden, here among the beech trees, with the late sunlight slanting through the copper-colored leaves. A squirrel, darting from the undergrowth, ran along the path before them, its cheeks stuffed with beechmast, its plumy tail quivering like a small glowing flame. When it stopped to look back at them with bright beady eyes, sitting up on its haunches, its tiny paws clasped to its breast as if in alarm, they stood still, laughing—a sound that sent the little creature off in a streak of russet brown fur, to shoot up the nearest tree trunk.

"They are mischievous little devils, but I haven't the heart to shoot them," Iain said, as they moved on.

"I can't imagine you killing anything," Susan told him fervently.

"Do I seem to you that soft?" His tone was wry. "I don't enjoy killing—but there are times when it has to be done. Those fat pigeons, for instance, who plunder my beans and peas . . . I shoot them by the dozen without turning a hair. And there was an old dog fox last spring harrying my lambs. I soon gave him his comeuppance!" He laughed. "Don't tell the local Master of Hounds!"

They had come through the wood now to a clearing, where sheep cropped the rough grass among the whin bushes. Iain spoke of his old sheep dog, Tanner, who had recently died. "I'd had him for twelve years. He was as useful as an extra hand around the place . . . and a good old pal: I miss him terribly."

Susan said softly, "It's bad enough losing a pet . . . but a dog that works with you the way these wonderful sheep dogs do . . . it must leave quite a gap!"

"It does," Iain agreed grimly. He had ordered another,

a young dog bred on the Cumberland Fells. But it wouldn't be the same as having old Tanner around. At least not at first. "Though you always get attached to them in the end," he confessed "You can't help it. They are so intelligent, so loyal—and such good company. Many a winter night I've spent out on the hills in lambing time, with only old Tanner along . . . and I never felt as if I were alone. He was as good as many a human . . . better than some!" He sighed nostalgically, and Susan at his side found herself picturing the scene vividly. The long dark night on the bleak hillside, the sheep with their newborn lambs in the rough hurdle shelters . . . and Iain with staff and storm lantern, a plaid around his shoulders, trudging from shelter to shelter—with the faithful Tanner at his heels.

They had come to the top of the hill now and stood on the summit looking down at the valley bathed in the clear evening light. Iain pointed out to her the boundaries of his estate. She caught the ring of pride in his tone—a man surveying the land he possessed. Looking up into his lean, strong face, she felt her pulse quicken. There was something about the moment that made Iain seem suddenly a little set apart. A man who owned the land on which he walked had a natural dignity that was rare—an indefinable quality rapidly vanishing from a world too highly mechanized, too ruthlessly organized.

She said gropingly, falteringly, "People huddled together in cities, Iain—they miss so much!"

He gave her a long, searching glance. "What made you think of that all of a sudden?"

"I don't know! The space here . . . the peace, the security; this feeling that the land you can see all around you belongs to you. It must be rather wonderful."

He gave a small dry shrug. "Not quite as wonderful as you imagine, perhaps. Farming is often more of a liability than a security nowadays. But you city folk are all the same—when you see the idyllic scene on a summer evening you think the farmer's life is all milk and honey!"

She felt chilled and rebuffed. Why was it that whenever she made some glowing comment on life at Glenelg, Iain flung it back at her—as if deliberately trying to disillusion her, make her see things in their most unfavorable light? Perhaps it was just his Scots mistrust of facile enthusiasm, his honest insistence upon facts being presented stark and unvarnished. But it was a bit discouraging.

When he spoke again it was to announce that it was close to suppertime, and that they'd better hurry home if they didn't want to get into Kirstie's bad books. "She hates having her cooking efforts spoiled by waiting," he explained. "Likes serving things on the dot"—a fact Susan had already discovered for herself.

It was a rushed and breathless journey back through the little wood, not conducive to conversation, and scurrying along, trying to keep up with Iain's long-legged strides, Susan felt oddly bleak and shut out.

When Jan returned from the hospital that evening she ran into the kitchen where Susan was helping Kirstie clear up after the meal. One look at her radiant face told them that the news of Tony was more hopeful. A brain specialist had been called in. "A Sir Somebody Treeves-Brown," Jan told them breathlessly. "He says Tony's prolonged unconsciousness is caused by pressure from the wound over his temple. There is no injury to the brain itself, and the pressure can be relieved by a minor operation—which this Sir Treeves himself is going to perform tomorrow. The ward nurse says I'm to give Tony a day or two to get over the operation—but she thinks he should be able to recognize me and talk to me a little by about Sunday. Oh, Susan, isn't it marvelous!" She flung her arms around her sister in an ecstasy of relief. After her long week of despair, her spirits had risen to wild heights at the first hint of better things.

Kirstie took a plate of roast meat and vegetables from the oven and set it on the table. "Maybe you'll eat your supper tonight, instead of giving most of it to Tibby, the cat," she remarked dryly.

"I'm ravenous," Jan assured her. The village bus didn't get her back from Edinburgh until after nine and her evening meal had to be kept hot for her. Tonight, for the first time, she ate it with zest, going over and over the good news. Tony's shoulder was knitting satisfactorily and his bruised ribs had healed.

"The nurse says he has a marvelous constitution," she rattled on happily. "By the way, they have realized he is *the* Tony Brampton, the society portrait painter." She made a small rueful grimace at Susan. "The newspapers have found out about his accident—through the police, I suppose. Anyway, a reporter called at the hospital this morning, asking all sorts of questions. The nurse told him Mr. Brampton was in Edinburgh to attend the festival, and asked me if that was right. I said it was." Jan shrugged resignedly.

"We're not broadcasting the full story to the world in general," Susan explained to Kirstie.

"You're very wise. A runaway marriage is naught to be proud of," Kirstie's tone was blunt. She glanced severely at Jan. "Oh, yes, Susan has told me all about it . . . the worry and distress you have been causing your parents. I know it's no business of mine," she added, as Jan colored.

"You'll be thinking, no doubt, I'm an old fogy who has forgotten what it is to be young. But youth is no excuse for blind selfishness. . . ."

Jan looked as if she were going to explode. "You've no right to judge me like this," she burst out. "There are times when one has to be selfish. You don't know anything about Tony and me. . . ."

"Maybe not," Kirstie agreed quietly. "But I know well enough that marriage is a gamble at the best of times, and a hole-in-the-corner marriage gets off to a bad start. I'd have little respect for a man who would lure a girl your age from her home in the face of her parents' wishes. He'd make a poor sort of husband, if you ask me."

"I'm not asking you," Jan said rudely.

There was an awkward silence. They all looked up with relief when Iain came in. He had disappeared after supper to the room he used as an office to catch up on some paper work.

"I've lost that damned questionnaire on crop rotation that came with this morning's mail," he announced in a goaded tone. "Did I leave it in here?" He caught sight of Jan and his frown of annoyance disappeared. "So you got back!" he welcomed her. "What's the news tonight?"

"Marvelous! They think Tony is going to be all right!" Joyfully she launched once more into the story of the illustrious brain surgeon who was to banish all her troubles with a wave of his scalpel. Was she being too optimistic, Susan wondered. But her mood was a characteristic swing from the depths to the heights. There were no half measures with Jan.

Sitting down at the table opposite her Iain watched her vivid, lovely face as she talked—crop rotation forgotten. She was wearing the new, coral jersey suit tonight, with a

brilliant scarf of vivid blue. The color called up by Kirstie's
rebuke still flamed in her cheeks and her brown eyes held
golden lights. "Think of it!" she exulted. "By Sunday
Tony should be almost his old self again. At any rate he'll
be able to talk to me—know I'm there with him!"

"That's grand," Iain murmured absently. "Best news
I've heard in a long while." But he wasn't thinking about
Tony, Susan felt. He couldn't take his eyes off Jan.
Tonight, in her glowing mood, her beauty had a luminous
quality. She seemed with her rich dark coloring like some
vivid, tropical flower in the quiet farm kitchen.

"Here's your questionnaire. It was in the soup tureen on
the dresser," Kirstie announced, slapping a long official
envelope down in front of Iain. "I must have put it there
when I was clearing the table after breakfast."

She waited for the reproaches that didn't come. Iain
merely stuffed the envelope into his pocket, with an
automatically mumbled, "Thanks." The form filling, in-
separable from modern farming, irked him beyond words.
Half of it was sheer bull, he had confided to Susan impatiently one day when Kirstie had sent her with a cup of
midmorning coffee to the small back room, once a butler's
pantry, that was his office. The state of his desk had
appalled her. He had obviously no idea of office routine.
Would he be offended, she had wondered, if she offered to
put things straight for him? Perhaps if she chose her moment carefully . . . men hated having their possessions
"tidied up."

She watched him now, heaving himself out of his chair,
obviously reluctant to go back to his clerking. He stood
hesitant a moment, towering over Jan, who glanced up at
him in unconscious provocation. Though she was totally
unaware of it, she had all the makings of an accomplished

flirt. Personable men titillated her, perhaps because her lively good looks attracted them and made them behave toward her with flattering attentiveness. And in an innocent way she enjoyed this very much.

"You'll not be making your usual trips to the hospital for a while, then," Iain worked it out.

"No, I've got to leave it till Sunday, the nurse says."

"Maybe in that case you'd like to step out a bit . . . see something of the festival—both of you. . . ?" He looked over at Susan as if she were an after thought. "I didn't like to suggest it before when things were so grim, but now that you're easier in your minds it might amuse you to come to our beanfeast on Saturday."

"Iain is dancing on the Fringe," Kirstie put in.

The two girls stared at her. Iain burst out laughing at their mystified faces. "She means I'm one of the humble mortals who make their contribution to the arts during festival time, by giving performances in the smaller halls and school rooms on the outskirts of the town. We're known as the Fringe. The Folk Song and Dance Society I belong to is holding a shindig up on Calton Hill on Saturday evening. After the performance we have a bit of a party among ourselves—to which we are allowed to invite guests. It ought to be fun. What about it?"

"We'd love to come!" Jan answered enthusiastically for both of them.

"Only that I've nothing to wear," Susan pointed out. She had left home with a minimum of luggage and apart from the trim tailored suit she had traveled in, possessed only a couple of cotton dresses.

"You can borrow something of mine," Jan assured her.

"That's settled then," Iain announced in a tone of satisfaction.

It wasn't until after they had got to bed that night that Susan began to face the full implications of Jan's good news. If Tony regained consciousness after his operation and was soon to be well on the way to recovery there would be problems to face, decisions to be taken. They would be back at the deadlock they had reached that hideous moment just before Tony stepped off the pavement under the oncoming van. Would he and Jan be any more reasonable about their marriage plans when the discussions were resumed? It was most unlikely.

Lying in the big four-poster bed, Susan stared into the darkness, listening to Jan's quiet breathing at her side. She had dropped off tonight the moment her head touched the pillow—convinced, poor child, that her troubles were practically over. But they weren't. They were only just beginning. Each time Susan phoned Moorings during the week gone by, her mother had urged that Jan must come home as soon as possible. The Harrowbys, indeed, and perhaps naturally enough, were inclined to regard Tony's accident as an intervention of Providence. It hadn't been easy to make them understand that it had, in fact, settled nothing. It had seemed to them obvious that both girls could now come back to Moorings—leaving ultimate decisions in the air. Brampton was safely in the hosptial, having the best of attention, no doubt—providing them all with a blessed respite during which Jan could be argued with, persuaded. . . . It had taken Susan quite a time to get it into their heads that nothing would induce her to leave Tony—ill and unconscious—but at last they had agreed that it would perhaps be unkind to expect it of her. But their patience would not last forever. A crisis of some kind was imminent.

Hopelessly, Susan tossed and turned, wondering what

the next few days would bring forth, and how she would face their challenge. It was impossible to tell how it would all turn out. Only one thing was certain—one way or another the problem of Jan and her Tony must be solved—and solved soon—and then their stay at Glenelg would come to an end.

CHAPTER EIGHT

ON SATURDAY there was a holiday feeling in the air. Iain drove the girls to Edinburgh when he made his morning trip to deliver the vegetables. Afterward he took them on a sight-seeing tour. "He'll make you a good guide," Kirstie had promised them the night before when the expedition had been planned. "There's little about the history of Edinburgh—its old tales and its old buildings—that Iain doesn't know." A statement he had modestly qualified.

"You'd need to be a walking encyclopaedia to hold that lot in your head!" he had declared. "And much of it you'd find pretty boring."

But there wasn't a dull moment in that bright Saturday forenoon. They started by walking through Princes Gardens, where Jan was childishly fascinated by the great floral clock that faithfully told the hour. Then they climbed the hill to the castle. Iain showed them the three rooms occupied by Mary, Queen of Scots, one of them little larger that a good-sized cupboard, where her only son, James, had been born. The small bare room seemed full of the echoes of "old unhappy, far-off days."

"I've always had a 'thing' about poor Mary, Queen of Scots," Jan said, touching a paneled wall with a reverent forefinger. "She was so lovely—and so unlucky!" In her golden brown eyes there lurked a shadow that told Susan she was identifying herself with the ill-fated queen. "If only these walls could speak!" she sighed romantically.

"They do their best," Iain pointed to the royal arms on the wainscoting, with the date of the baby's birth, and the strange old prayer beneath it, written in an archaic script difficult to make out.

"Lord Jesu Chryst that crownit was with thornise," it began, "Preserve the Birth quhais Badgie heir is borne. . . ."

"What on earth does it mean?" Jan pondered, lingering over the ancient words, and Iain told them how Mary when showing the new baby to its father, Darnley, was supposed to have said, very simply and touchingly: 'My Lord, God hath given us a son.'

There was a suspicion of tears in Jan's eyes as they moved on to the banqueting hall with its stained glass windows and imposing show of armor. But they couldn't attempt to "do" the entire castle in one day, Iain reminded them. There was the Royal Mile to be explored, with its fabulous old houses, its "wynds" and closes—all of them saturated in history. Names and dates and anecdotes tripped off Iain's tongue. In St. Giles Cathedral they stood before the memorial of Robert Louis Stevenson reading his well-known "Requiem"—"Home is the sailor, home from the sea. And the hunter home from the hill."

"It all makes me feel so small and insignificant," Susan burst out, overpowered by the weight of the centuries. "All these wonderful people who lived and loved . . . and then just faded from the scene to become ghosts to enliven a tourist's holiday!"

Iain laughed, took her arm companionably and told her that what she needed was a nice cup of coffee. They had done enough sight-seeing for one day. But they were still pursued by history, for the coffee-house to which they went had once been a famous tavern, frequented, if legend was to be believed, by a glittering list of notorieties, from the roistering Bothwells to Sir Walter Scott.

Jan left them for a few moments to make her daily phone call to the hospital. The operation on Tony was safely over, but all she could glean that morning from the routine report by the hall porter was that Mr. Brampton was "Very comfortable," and would be able to have visitors the following day. It was enough to keep her spirits high.

On the way home in the station wagon she sang to herself in a soft, sweet undertone . . . snatches of popular songs, and finally a quaint old ballad Susan had never heard her sing before.

"Sing it properly," Iain begged. "You've a bonny voice and its a bonny wee song by the sound of it."

With an odd sidelong glance at Susan, Jan said a little defiantly, "All right, you asked for it!"

In her lilting voice with its hint of contralto richness she began:

> My mother said that I never should play
>   with the gypsies in the wood.
> The wood was dark, the grass was green. In
>   came Sally with her tambourine.
> I went to the sea—no ship to get across
> I paid ten shillings for a blind white horse.
> I up on his back and was off in a crack!
> Sally, tell my mother I shall never come back!

There was a strained little silence when the song ended. Then Jan laughed. "The signature tune for the frustrated but undefeated Bramptons!" she said.

"That's a pretty ancient traditional song, I should think . . ." Iain offered awkwardly after a moment.

"About an ancient traditional family quarrel," Jan returned, cheerfully. "And I bet Sally and her tambourine were on the losing side!"

Susan said nothing. There was nothing she could say. Jan in this mood frightened her. There was a ruthless quality in her makeup that was entirely foreign to Susan's more gentle nature. She is stronger than I am, she thought; stronger than any of us . . . even father. In the pitched battle that lay ahead it was not Jan who would be broken.

Back at Glenelg she dominated the luncheon table, entertaining Kirstie with a colorful account of the morning's expedition. "I had no idea," she said mischievously, "that the Scots were such a wild lot! Did you know that the elegant young lady who later became the Duchess of Gordon once rode on the back of a sow all the way down the High Street, her sister tearing along behind her, driving the animal along with mighty whacks on its behind! Another was the aristocratic Miss Eglintoune who used to fill her kettle at an old well in the close to make tea for her boyfriends."

"Iain had no business to be filling your head with such nonsense," Kirstie remarked primly. "I'm ashamed of ye if ye got nothing more elevating than that out of your morning!"

"Oh, but we did," Jan assured her with a giggle. "It was all most instructive." She glance provocatively at Iain. He returned her look levelly, his hazel eyes hard.

"There's times, young Jan," he said coolly, "when what you need isn't instruction—but a good spanking on that place the Lord designed for that purpose!"

"Really, Iain!" Kirstie gasped, outraged. But Jan only

looked more pleased with herself than ever, and as soon as
the meal was over, leaving Susan to help with the dishes,
she announced that she was going out to make a sketch of
the house with the beech woods rising behind it.

Running upstairs to fetch easel and paints she was singing the rebellious song again.

I went to the sea—no ship to get across;
  I paid ten shillings for a blind white horse. . . .

But in spite of her wild mood Susan was glad to see her
taking an interest in her painting once more. During the
days Tony lay unconscious she had refused all suggestions
that it might be a way of passing the anxious hours. For the
whole of that troubled week she had had no heart for her
work. Susan had never known her to go so long without a
brush or pencil in her hand.

Nor, as it turned out, did today's effort last very long.
Going upstairs to her bedroom when the dishes were done,
Susan went over the window, wondering how the painting
was coming along. But the easel set up on the terrace was
deserted and Jan, she saw, was walking in the kitchen
garden at Iain's side. Together they stooped over the
strawberry bed, pausing to admire the espaliered nectarines—Iain's special pride. It was his first attempt to
grow the fruit, and Kirstie had jokingly declared that he
counted the nectarines each day and would never have the
heart to pick them. But now Susan saw him lift the net that
protected them from the birds and recklessly select two or
three of the ripest for Jan to eat—which she proceeded to
do, very prettily—Iain watching her in an absurdly
gratified way. He had apparently quite forgiven her for her
flippant account of their sight-seeing morning.

With a stifled sigh, Susan settled down to her sewing. She was shortening the skirt of the dress Jan had loaned her for the evening; a demure maize-colored silk that she herself had picked out, because it was one of the quieter items of Jan's rather flamboyant wardrobe. She had an exotic taste in clothes and with her height and vivid coloring could carry off the most daring confections. Tonight she was to wear one of her trousseau dresses, a full-skirted white silk patterned with big scarlet poppies, and a scarlet stole to match. She was going to feel pretty mousy in comparison, Susan thought, stitching away at the pale yellow skirt.

Later when they were dressing, Jan eyed her sister critically. "You need a spot of something to cheer that dress up," she pronounced, and produced a string of topaz beads that helped a little, but the colors were wrong for Susan with her blue gray eyes and fair hair. However, there was nothing to be done about it—she had long ago ceased to compete with Jan when it came to clothes.

They went out onto the galleried landing, Jan proud as a gypsy queen in her finery, her dark head held high—knowing she was looking her best tonight and disdaining the knowledge, for Tony was not here to see her. She had put on her gay clothes in a mood that was half-defiant—a challenge to fate. After the long days of dread and despair there was hope once more in her heart and she was a little drunk with its sweetness.

As she swept down the white staircase, Kirstie, awaiting them in the hall, gave an audible gasp at the sight of her. Then Iain appeared in kilt and jerkin, and it was Jan's turn to gasp. Susan, behind her, felt a catch at her heart. She had never before seen Iain in national costume, and its

magnificence overwhelmed her—MacDowell of the Clan
MacDowell, wearing his family tartan.

"Oh, Iain, what splendor!" In rapt delight Jan stood
before him her hands clasped to her breast. He laughed
down at her in gentle amusement. "You're pretty splen-
did yourself!"

"But the lace cuffs and jabot, the silver buttons and
buckles, the darling little velvet coat!" Jan enumerated.
"You're just like some gorgeous creature out of an
eighteenth-century painting . . . when men weren't afraid
to dress up. The kilt is quite heavenly!"

"All right if you have the legs for it," Kirstie put in
waspishly.

"And Iain *has*," Jan affirmed with vigor.

Kirstie gave her an oblique glance, and swept out to the
waiting station wagon. She was wearing a limp, flowered
voile, that emphasized her scragginess. "You and I will sit
in the back with the vegetable sacks, Susan." She arranged
it. "Let the silks and velvets go in front." Was there a hint
of a sneer in her tone? Jan's flamboyant dress with its low-
cut bodice was probably a bit too much for, her, Susan
thought uneasily. So far, Kirstie had been kindness itself to
Jan—subdued by trouble. But now that prospects were
brighter the real Jan was beginning to emerge—
headstrong, impulsive, impatient of restraint. There would
be fireworks when Tony came back into the picture.
Kirstie, it was clear, would countenance no runaway marriage from Glenelg! With a suppressed sigh, Susan decided
there was no use meeting complications halfway and
resolutely switched her thoughts to the gaieties ahead.

They arrived at Calton Hill in good time. When they got
out of the car Iain made them stand a moment to look

across the valley to the towers of Holyrood Palace, with
Arthur's Seat and Salisbury Crags vivid as a painted
backdrop behind them. Built like Rome on its hills, the city
rose around them on all sides—a rugged line of crests and
rooftops against the evening sky. The Athenian pillar of
the old observatory caught Jan's eye. There were so many
touches of Greek architecture in Edinburgh, she said. And
Iain told her proudly it had been called "the Athens of the
North."

But people were already pouring into the school hall.
"We'll need to claim our seats," Kirstie pronounced fussily.
Iain left them to go in by the green room door. Through a
wide uncurtained window Susan caught a glimpse of girl
performers putting last minute touches to their makeup.
They all wore the same kind of white evening dresses, with
vivid tartan sashes pinned to one shoulder.

In the hall specatators sat on tiers of seats arranged
around a long oval of space that served as a stage. Light
streamed down on the honey-colored floor, a pool of pale
gold on which the dancers wove their intricate patterns.
From an upper gallery three fiddlers and a melodian player
poured out the lilting Scots airs, sad and gay—wild as the
winds that blew through the heather. There were reels and
jigs, and a strathspey gentle as a minuet. At the end of each
dance the men in their velvet and laces bowed to the white
clad girls, who answered with sweeping curtsies. It was all
grace and dignity, curiously controlled in an old-world
way, until in the middle of a breathless Highland reel the
men lifted their voices in the ancient traditional cry. Again
and again it rang out, primitive in its savagery. Susan felt
her blood tingle.

The floor was cleared then and the lights dimmed. In a
single spotlight Iain stood alone, two swords held high

above his head. The melodian played a challenging chord and burst into a wild flood of music. Laying the swords in a cross at his feet Iain danced between the glittering blades. His face was tranced and set, his head erect. It was a strangely formal dance, complicated and swift—yet carried out with a studied hauteur. Like some ancient ritual of war, Susan thought. The victory dance of a clan leader exulting over fallen foes. It seemed to take her away into a distant place and time, when all men were heroic, all battles tales of chivalry.

Jan, at her side, leaned forward in her seat, her glance fixed on Iain, enthralled. "Isn't he fabulous, Sue!" she whispered.

Susan felt her throat swell. An intolerable pain shot through her. *I am in love with him,* she thought helplessly, utterly and head over heels in love. There was no use trying to hide it from herself any longer. On a tide of bittersweetness the knowledge flooded her heart. Ever since that day they had met in the train she had been evading it, unable to believe that love could come like this. A look, a smile, a moment shared—and the whole face of her world had changed. Just like they said in the romantic songs and poems. Though in the poems and songs it always happened to two people simultaneously. Iain liked her company, enjoyed talking to her about his work and his interests . . . but there was no sign that she meant anything more to him than any other girl.

His sword dance had ended now—he stood with the blades upraised, acknowledging the storm of applause. Did she imagine that he glanced straight up to where she was sitting? But if he smiled and gestured a little, it was as much for Kirstie and Jan as for herself. Then he was gone and the houselights came on. Susan shrank from their brilliance, longing suddenly to hide herself, fearful that her secret might show in her face. To love unasked, unsought . . . throw everything you had into a vacuum of kindly indifference—could anything be more foolish?

The choir, unaccompanied, began singing the "Eriskay Love Lilt,"—tender, nostalgic, a soft rising and falling of sound, gentle as the swelling tide of a summer sea. Tears filled her eyes—it was more than she could bear—and she was glad when the music came to an end and with it the first part of the evening's program. There was a general movement, the audience streaming out into the courtyard while tables were laid for the buffet supper that was to follow.

It was almost dark now—that luminous half-light that seemed to linger in these latitudes until close to midnight. Wanting to be alone, Susan drifted away from Kirstie and Jan, and presently discovered with a start of surprise that Iain was beside her. He put a masterful hand on her arm and led her out onto the hill road. She could feel her pulse racing under his touch and feared he would hear the thundering of her heart. In the western sky a young moon sailed serenely.

"Let's wish on it!" Iain said.

They stood looking up at the remote sickle of silver. Susan didn't dare to put her wish into words—even in her inmost mind. But her whole soul ached with the longing for one word or look or sign from Iain that would echo her own inarticulate yearning. Covertly she glanced at his absorbed, uplifted face. *He is wishing for good weather for the crops,* she thought sadly, *or for a nice fat price for his tomatoes!* But whatever it was, he wasn't telling! They walked on for a while in silence and when they reached a bend in the road he pointed out to her the crest of land ris-

ing above them, that had once been the site of a notorious
prison. Some years ago it had been demolished, and its
stones removed to build a reservoir in a valley oddly named
Hopes.

"Hopes Reservoir," he said, "is one of our local beauty
spots. It is not far from Glenelg. One day I must take you
there, it is only about half an hour's walk from the house,
along the banks of our little burn."

As they turned to go back to the hall she found herself
treasuring the casually made promise. Would he ever think
of it again? Hopes Reservoir—the name lingered in her
mind. There was a hint of symbolism about it that pleased
her. A place where the waters, gathered from the high hills,
rested—cradled by the stones that had once housed
hopeless men. Was there a message for her here—a hint
that fate, even when life was at its most baffling, could
produce twists and turns in circumstances that made the
way clear again? But she was being morbidly introspective,
she told herself sharply—seeing herself and her small problems as the center of the universe!

"Where have you two been hiding yourselves?" Jan
greeted them accusingly when they got back to the hall.
The buffet supper was well under way, and Iain was at
once claimed by a group of girls in white dresses and gay
plaids. He introduced Jan and Susan. Several young men
in kilts and velvet jerkins joined them, and there was an interval of animated chatter and harmless banter as coffee
cups circulated and sandwiches and cakes were passed
around. Susan did her best to join in, but it all seemed
curiously dreamlike and unreal.

The dancing, when it began, proved to be a program of
set reels and lancers. "I'm no good at this sort of thing,"
she told Iain—quite truthfully, for she was more ac-

customed to conventional ballroom dancing. But she was glad of the excuse to withdraw, seized suddenly by an agonizing fit of shyness. The thought of giving herself up to Iain's arms out there on the shining oval of floor filled her with a strange terror she couldn't define—only that she knew she couldn't have borne it tonight. So she slipped away to find Kirstie, who was looking rather lonely and neglected among the wallflowers sprinkled around the galleried seats. Together they watched Jan in her poppy-splashed dress weaving her way through the complicated mazes with a variety of partners. But it was most often with Iain that she danced.

"There's not much sign that she's fretting for the absent sweetheart tonight!" Kirstie remarked, eyeing the gaily whirling figure a little sourly. It was true enough. Jan seemed intoxicated with her own happiness this evening, lifting her lovely, laughing face to Iain as he swung her through the labyrinth of the final set of lancers. Light-footed and confident, she followed his lead with flawless ease. Even in that assembly of expert dancers they stood out as a strikingly handsome couple. They danced together as if they were made for each other, Susan thought with a twinge of pain.

In the car going home she took her place by his side—as if it were her right; not waiting this time for Kirstie to arrange it. Susan in the back among the empty vegetable sacks listened to her chattering comments on the evening's entertainment. The plaids the Scottish girls had worn filled her with envy, she declared. "All those gorgeous rich colors draped over the white dresses are so effective. They leave an ordinary evening dress just nowhere. It's . . . unfair competition." She gave Iain a sidelong glance, subtly challenging. "I wish I had the right to wear a tartan!" she sighed.

"You'd better marry a Scotsman then," he chaffed her.

She laughed up at him, softly, provocatively. "That's quite an idea, Mr. MacDowell!" The drawled-out words held a hint of mockery. "I'll have to think it over."

Susan saw him turn sharply and look down at her in an odd, arrested way. His face, caught in the glare of a streetlight, seemed curiously young and defenseless at that moment, and there was no answering laughter in his eyes.

CHAPTER NINE

THEY WOKE next morning to gray skies and a thin drizzling rain. Jan's optimistic mood had evaporated. Sunday visiting hours at the hospital were from two until four, and as the morning wore on she grew more and more nervous.

"Supposing the operation hasn't been as successful as they say?" she speculated desolately to Susan. "Do you think you could bear to come with me this afternoon? I don't think I can face it alone."

"Of course, I'll come with you," Susan agreed at once, glad that Jan had suggested it. A great deal might depend on today's visit. If Tony were fully in possession of his senses once more, all sorts of situations could arise. For one thing, Susan could well imagine him demanding to be moved from the hospital. How long would he be convalescing, she wondered. It was sad that he had no family or friends to turn to at such a time; that there was no one to take care of him in the interval of being nursed back to complete health—only Jan. It was going to be a pretty difficult situation, Susan told herself grimly.

Kirstie, preparing a special Sunday lunch, was a little put out when she realized they would have to leave the house before one o'clock in order to catch the local bus.

"What an old fuss pot she is!" Jan grumbled, as they hurried down the lane to the village. "As though Sunday lunches mattered at a moment like this!"

Once more Susan wondered how long Jan and Kirstie would succeed in living in the same house without a major upheaval. Their natures and outlooks were poles apart.

In the bus Jan's spirits rose again. By the time they reached the hopsital she was in a state of tremulous expectancy, and was scarcely able to contain herself when she found they had to wait in a line of patients' visitors until the clock struck two. But at last they were hurrying down the now familiar, green-washed corridor.

The men's surgical ward seemed to Susan vast and bewildering, but Jan made confidently for Tony's screened bed at the far end of the long bright room. He was sitting up, drinking a glass of fruit juice. His beard had been shaved off. For a moment this took Susan so much aback that she could not think of anything else. It made him look much younger . . . and nicer, she thought. He had a good strong jawline, she discovered with interest, and a firm well-shaped mouth. A narrow adhesive dressing on his brow was the only sign of his injury. If he seemed a little wan and fragile that was only to be expected after all he had been through.

"How nice of you to come and see me," he said with a formal little smile. "The nurse told me she thought I might have some visitors this afternoon . . . though I'm afraid the name she mentioned conveyed very little to me. . . ."

"Tony!" Jan gasped. She sank down by the bedside on her knees, as though her legs had given way under her. "Don't you recognize me, darling?" she begged.

The formal smile became a little more set. "Ought I to?" Tony murmured. He glanced appealingly at Susan, as if hoping she might help him to clear up the mystery. "I'm afraid I've never had the pleasure of meeting either of you before . . . but I do think it is kind of you to have come to see me. And if you can tell me something of what happened just before my accident I'll be eternally grateful! It seems I had come to Edinburgh to visit the festival—''

"Oh, Tony!" Jan cried in a stunned, incredulous way.

A nurse appeared from behind the screen. She looked a little flustered. "The ward nurse would like to see you in her office, Miss Harrowby," she said, with a hurried glance at the kneeling, distraught Jan. She turned to Susan. "Perhaps you'd better both come."

Susan helped Jan to her feet. "We'll be back," she called brightly to Tony, as she led Jan away. It seemed an endless journey down the long ward. Jan walked as though she moved in a dream, her face chalk white, her dark eyes dilated.

There was a cosy, chintzy air about the small glassed-in office, and there were flowers on the desk where the ward nurse sat writing. She rose to greet them, a tall authoritative woman with a kindly smile. "I meant to waylay you before you got as far as the ward," she told Jan. "I'm afraid it will have been a bit of a shock to you to find Mr. Brampton doesn't remember you."

Jan said brokenly, "I . . . just can't believe it! Does it mean the operation hasn't been any good after all?"

"Oh, no—it has been completely successful, and you'll be relieved to hear there is no *physical* damage to the brain."

"But . . . some other kind of damage?" Jan said. She gulped down what sounded like a strangled sob.

"My sister and Mr. Brampton were very close friends," Susan felt urged to explain. "She was studying painting under his tuition."

"I see. . . ." The nurse looked searchingly into Jan's stricken face, as if she were trying to get at the true facts of the situation. She touched the girl's shoulder gently. "You must give Mr. Brampton time, my dear. After all, it is early days yet. It is something that he has regained consciousness, and that he is beginning to piece things together again. He speaks of his studio in Paris . . . seems to think he came here straight from there."

"But he came from Moorings, in Sussex," Jan burst out. "He was living in a hotel there near our home. I worked with him in his studio at Oakford. . . ."

The nurse said, "Well let him get around to all that in his own time. I sent for you to warn you that he mustn't be hurried or forced in any way. Sometimes in these cases of shock following on head injury, the amnesia—loss of memory, that is—is a subconscious defense mechanism. The patient may be deliberately shutting out circumstances that are painful to him."

"You mean Tony is forgetting me on purpose?" Jan blurted incredulously.

The nurse smiled. "I wouldn't put it quite like that. But if anything about his stay in Moorings, or his journey to Edinburgh happened to be a worry to him, he may unconsciously suppress it until he feels more able to cope with it. And you must let him suppress it. Any attempt to jolt him into remembering things he doesn't want to remember, may only drive him more deeply into his amnesia. Answer any questions he asks you, of course, otherwise the more impersonal you keep it the better."

"How long do you think he will remain in this state?" Susan hazarded. Jan seemed incapable of speech.

The nurse shook her neat white-coiffed head. "It's impossible to say. The condition might clear up in a day or two, or it might persist for weeks. Meanwhile, do come in and see him as often as you can—as long as you are in Edinburgh.

"The stimulus of having visitors is good for him. Providing," she added warningly, "there is no sense of strain." She was ushering them out as she spoke.

In the corridor Jan stood with her face buried in her hands. "I can't go back to the ward, Susan," she said thickly. "I . . . *can't*! Tony looking at me with those cold distant eyes as if I were a blank stranger! I just can't bear it—I'll die!" The last words trailed away into a hysterical sob.

Susan's heart ached with pity, but she forced herself to speak bracingly, telling Jan to pull herself together. "It's only about forty-eight hours since his operation," she reminded her. "Naturally he's still a bit hazy. And he needs your help. The nurse said he did. You'd never forgive yourself if you walked out on him now—just because not being recognized upsets you."

Jan lifted her stricken face, faint hope in her tearful eyes, "If you think I can really help him. . . ."

"Of course you can. His memory may clear at any moment, as the nurse said. And the more he sees of you, the quicker it will happen," Susan urged.

Jan straightened her shoulders and went back to the ward.

They spent an uncomfortable quarter of an hour there. Tony was polite and faintly embarrassed. The fact that he was expected to know why they were there obviously annoyed him. When he apologized again for his obtuseness he sounded impatient rather than regretful.

"It doesn't matter in the least," Susan assured him.

He cast a speculative glance at Jan. "You weren't one of the students at the Beaux Arts in Paris, were you?"

"No, I was studying at the Oakford School of Art . . . near Moorings," Jan said and held her breath, waiting for her words to ring a bell.

But Tony shook his head. "Moorings?" he echoed vaguely. "Sorry, it doesn't mean a thing to me . . . never heard of the place." He was beginning to look tired and strained, and remembering the nurse's injunctions Susan brought the visit to an end.

Going home in the bus Jan had a struggle to hold back the tears. "I can't imagine any kind of accident making *me* forget *him*," she choked.

"That's ridiculous," Susan scolded cheerfully. "You don't know what you'd be like if you had been run over by a tradesman's van and then had a head operation on top of it. But I wish," she added a little doubtfully, "that the nurse hadn't gone into all those details about subconscious defense mechanisms. I'm sure she would not have been so explicit if she had realized how it would hurt you. Anyway, it was all supposition."

"But it could so easily be true," Jan said in a small voice. "Tony *was* worried just before his accident—because you had followed us to Edinburgh. . . . And there was that unfortunate remark of yours about dad taking legal proceedings against us."

Susan winced. "I *had* to warn you," she defended herself. "I couldn't let Tony rush off with you into the blue without letting him know what he was up against."

"I know you couldn't," Jan conceded miserably. "The whole thing is a most ghastly mess."

"It will all come right if you have patience," Susan urged with more desperation than conviction.

Jan gave her a withering look. "How can it? You know what dad is like when he digs his heels in! But I don't care . . . he can send me to prison if he likes!" She gave a pathetic gulp. "I could bear anything . . . anything in the world, if only Tony remembered our love for one another. But to have him going on as if he'd never seen me before . . .

and he looks so different without his beard!'' Two large tears rolled down her cheeks.

Susan suppressed a smile. Poor little Jan—she was such a babe, after all, mourning for Tony's lost love and his lost beard all in the same breath. ''They had to shave it off for his operation, I suppose,'' she pointed out. ''You know how mad they are on hygiene in hospitals—it's a wonder they didn't shave his whole head!''

Jan gave a watery little giggle.

Susan tucked a hand through her arm. ''Cheer up, old girl! Tony's beard will grow again and his memory will come back . . . and then we'll have to decide what you are going to do next. I'll tell you what—go and see him tomorrow, and take his knapsack. There may be things in it he needs, and who knows, the sight of his familiar possessions may work a miracle.''

It was an inspired suggestion. Jan seized on it and wiped her eyes. There were all sorts of vital reminders in that knapsack—Tony's diary, a half-filled sketchbook, and a letter from an art magazine in New York inviting him to write an article on Italian fifteenth-century painting. Surely one or all of those things would remind him of the weeks he had mislaid!

By the time they got back to Glenelg she had recovered at least her outward composure, and ran up to her room to remove all traces of her tears, before joining the others for tea . . . served formally in the drawing room today, because it was Sunday.

Kirstie was pleased to see them home earlier than she had expected. ''You'll be able to make up for the way you rushed through your lunch,'' she declared, bringing a dish of freshly baked hot scones from the kitchen. There was new raspberry jam to go with them, and an assortment of homemade cookies and sandwiches. The best china had been brought out. The rain had caused a considerable drop in temperature and a fire of logs had been lighted on the beautiful Adam hearth. Susan couldn't help exclaiming how lovely it all looked. Hurriedly, while Jan was still out of the room, she told them all that had happened at the hospital. She saw Iain's·lean face tighten as he listened. "Poor Jan," he said in a low, almost angry tone. "She doesn't have much luck, does she?"

He was specially attentive to her throughout the meal, pressing her to eat. Nobody mentioned Tony's lapse of memory, but Kirstie was once more gentle and sympathetic in her manner toward Jan. It was an ill wind that blew nobody any good, Susan thought wryly. As long as Jan was in trouble Kirstie would be kindly disposed toward her.

After tea Iain asked Jan if she would like to go for a stroll. "I'll take you up the valley as far as the reservoir," he offered. "It's a bonny walk."

Susan felt splinters of ice in her heart as she watched them set out. Iain might have asked her to go with them . . . but apparently he had already forgotten his promise of the night before. It was Jan now who was to be shown the lake of shining water enclosed by the walls of the old dismantled jail.

She turned from the window to clear the tea table, and saw that Kirstie, too, was watching Jan and Iain walking down the driveway. "Off he goes, without a thought of the garden stuff waiting to be picked and packed for the early morning delivery!" she said with a short harsh laugh. "Poor Iain! He's got it badly, hasn't he? But I suppose it's only to be expected. Jan is just the type to bowl him over: pretty and appealing and down on her luck—it's more than his bump of chivalry could resist."

So she hadn't imagined Iain's growing infatuation for

Jan, Susan thought as she carried the tray through to the kitchen; Kirstie, too, had noticed it—with obvious disapproval. Not that she need worry: Jan was completely wrapped up in Tony. But supposing Tony faded out of the picture—as he so easily might. It was indeed difficult to see what else he could do, ultimately, if Dr. Harrowby decided to exercise his legal rights over his daughter. He would approve of Iain, Susan thought bleakly. There wouldn't be all this parental fuss about Jan being under age if it was a man like Iain who had asked for her. Nor would there be any question of a hurried marriage. Iain would be content to wait . . . until Jan was twenty-one if necessary. He would woo her patiently, doggedly—and it wasn't hard to imagine her turning to him in the end for comfort. Already she was very much attracted to him. Susan remembered the look on her face as she watched him last night doing the sword dance.

In a haze of misery she began to wash the dishes. She was being an idiot, she told herself, working herself up over a situation that didn't yet exist. It was quite bad enough to have fallen in love with Iain unasked and unwanted, without imagining all these fresh complications about Jan. Being jealous of her own sister was the final humiliation!

THE WEATHER now seemed to have broken permanently. For two days it rained steadily. Jan got wet through on her evening visits to the hospital. "If only I had the time to take her in the car!" Susan overheard Iain say to Kirstie.

"Well, you haven't," Kirstie had responded sharply. "Who is going to prepare the vegetable orders if you go gadding off? The evening hours are the busiest of your day. She's well clad and well shod, a drop of rain won't hurt her."

But she came home night after night, tired and bedraggled and dispirited. Iain's concern for her was increasingly apparent—though there was little he could do to express it, Susan concluded. At the moment Jan seemed hardly aware of him, her whole soul concentrated on Tony—who continued to treat her as a kindly, rather interfering stranger whose ministrations he couldn't understand. The knapsack hadn't helped at all—he had flung it into his bedside locker, refusing to show any interest in its contents.

"And the nurse watches me like a hawk," Jan grumbled. "Hardly leaves me alone with Tony a moment, for fear I shall say something to upset him. She obviously regards me as an overgrown schoolgirl with a crush on the art master. It's devastating, Sue. I can't stand much more of it!"

"Maybe it would be better to give up your visits for a while," Susan ventured. "When Tony's memory clears he'll send for you quickly enough . . . and you could wait for that just as well at home."

Jan rounded on her. They were getting ready for bed in the shadowy lamplit bedroom. "Do you mean go back to Moorings?" she cried in outrage.

"It may be weeks before Tony recovers from his amnesia," Susan pointed out. "We can't expect Kirstie and Iain to keep us here indefinitely. We ought to go home, Jan." If only Jan knew what the suggestion cost her! But it was a pretty obvious one.

Jan brushed her hair for a while in grim silence, then she said in an ominously quiet tone, "You go home if you want to. I'm staying till Tony is better. If you think the MacDowells are tired of having me I can get a room in Edinburgh."

"How will you pay for it?" Susan demanded practically. "It may be ages before Tony is fit to leave the hospital."

"I'll get a job," Jan declared. "Dish washing, waitressing . . . anything; just as long as I can see Tony every day. The nurse says that in cases like this the slightest jog to the memory can bring everything flooding back. It's simply a matter of hitting on the right thing—the missing link, so to speak."

"I must say it sounds a bit dicey," Susan murmured doubtfully.

Jan picked up her chiffon honeymoon nightie with an absentminded air. "If I could just have him to myself long enough, I'd try something drastic," she mused.

"Such as?" Susan prompted.

"Telling him right out that we came up to Edinburgh to be married," Jan announced defiantly. "There are lots of things I could say to make him remember. Look, Sue . . ." she turned to her sister appealingly. "Why don't you come with me tomorrow? You could keep that gorgon of a nurse talking in her office on some pretext or other while I get to work on Tony. . . ."

"It is afternoon visiting hours, being Wednesday," she urged, as Susan hesitated. "That means you'd be back in plenty of time for supper. I know Kirstie fusses when we miss meals. . . ."

"All right," Susan agreed a little dubiously. "I'll come. But if you say anything to upset Tony you'll never be allowed to visit him again."

"I'll take a chance on that," Jan muttered through set teeth. "Doctors and nurses don't know everything. Maybe all Tony is waiting for is a good big hug and a kiss, poor lamb!"

She could be right, Susan thought. At all events there didn't seem any harm in trying this simple remedy!

It was still raining the next morning. After breakfast

Susan retired to the little office. Iain had given her grudg-
ing permission to sort out the records and farming
magazines stacked on the floor.

"It's in a hopeless state of confusion," he had admitted,
and added not very gallantly that he didn't suppose she
could make matters worse than they were. "Papers and
documents seem to have a perverse life of their own," he
grumbled. "There's no controlling them."

But already Susan's experienced touch had worked
wonders in the chaos. Today she had decided to oil and
clean the neglected typewriter, and she was busy changing
the worn-out ribbon when Kirstie came in with the morning mail. There were two letters for Susan—one from her
mother and one that had been readdressed by the
housekeeper of her London apartment.

She opened her mother's first. The doctor had managed
to get hold of a locum tenens for a few days, Mrs. Harrowby wrote, and with Bridget safely back at her boarding
school there was nothing to hinder them having a short
holiday. They were driving up to Edinburgh by easy stages
and hoped to arrive on Thursday. The letter continued:

Your reports of Tony Brampton's condition are most
disquieting, and we are anxious to see for ourselves
just how things are. We can bring you both back with
us on Friday. Jan must realize by now that the whole
foolish affair is fizzling out . . . and thank God it is so.
Please tell your kind Miss MacDowell that we should
not dream of putting her out any further, and have
reserved a room at the Waverley Hotel for Thursday
night.

Susan's heart ached as she laid the letter down. Having

the date of her departure from Glenelg actually fixed, filled her with a strange sense of panic. It was as if her very life were being threatened. Which, of course, was ridiculous! It was the most natural thing in the world for their parents to have decided to come, and it would relieve her of all future responsibility for Jan. She ought to be glad, Susan told herself sternly. She *was* glad. . . .

But as she opened the second letter her fingers fumbled, and her eyes were so misty that for a moment she couldn't make out the figures on the pink check that tumbled out. The salary due to her from her London office . . . and a note from old Mr. Digby telling her her position in the firm was still open to her if she cared to return! Incredulously she read on: "I was somewhat hasty in dismissing you, but I trust you will reconsider the matter, and I shall be glad if you will resume your duties as soon as possible."

Astonishment and a feeling of triumph, momentarily lightened Susan's heavy heart. The summary dismissal had rankled . . . but she had never expected to see crusty old Mr. Digby eating humble pie! She was smiling to herself at the thought of it when Iain walked in.

"I've just remembered there's a form concerning sheep dipping that has to go off today," he announced. "Do you happen to know where it is?"

She lifted it out of the In basket she had organized.

He gazed at her in admiration. "Susan you're a marvel!" Seating himself opposite her, he began to fill in the form. "How did I ever live without you?" he murmured, a little absently as he scribbled away.

If only he meant that, Susan thought bleakly. She looked at the dark head bent over the desk, noticing how the close-cropped hair grew in a little peak above his forehead. Hungrily she studied the lean intent face, as if she would fix it in her memory for all time—the strong line of mouth and jaw, the trick he had of lifting one eyebrow when he was absorbed. There were freckles on the bridge of his nose, she discovered, and his lashes were long and thick and dark—much too beautiful for a man's.

As if aware of her scrutiny he glanced up. "You were looking remarkably pleased with yourself just now when I walked in. I see you've had some mail. . . ." With frank curiosity he eyed the newly opened envelopes and blatantly pink check lying beside the typewriter.

Susan picked up the check and waved it like a small triumphal banner. "I've got my old job back again. The boss has actually written to apologize for sacking me and invited me to start work again as soon as I like." She spoke with elation, still gloating over old Mr. Digby's comedown, hardly noticing the ominous silence into which the words dropped, nor did she see the sudden steely glint in Iain's eyes.

"When do you plan to begin?" he snapped.

"As soon as possible, I suppose," Susan answered, and because she hated the thought of it forced herself to add brightly, "Everything is really fitting in splendidly. My mother has written this morning to say my father has managed to get a few days off and they're driving up to take us home. They'll be here on Thursday and want us to be ready to leave by Friday—"

"So it's all arranged!" Iain burst out angrily. "The bright lights of London calling! You can't wait to get back to them, can you?"

She was amazed at his bitterness. It was as though she had offered him some personal affront. "It has nothing to do with bright lights," she protested. "Simply that I've got my living to earn . . . and this job of mine in London is interesting . . . well paid . . . the only thing I've been trained for. . . ." She broke off, seeing the hurt in his eyes deepen. "It's not that I *want* to go from here," she faltered. "Please, don't think that! Kirstie and you have been very kind. I've . . . loved every minute of it. . . ."

"I know!" He gave her a grim nod. "It's all very amusing and quaint at Glenelg . . . all right for a brief holiday, but not the sort of place you'd dream of burying yourself in for keeps."

"But there's no question of such a thing!" His air of reproach struck her as completely unreasonable. Provincial touchiness, she concluded. It couldn't be anything else. He thought she found Glenelg dull in comparison with London. If only he knew how far from the truth he was!

"Of course there's no question of it," he was saying. His hands clenching the desk were white at the knuckles. "I've realized that all along." With drawn dark brows he scowled at her—then suddenly he shook his broad shoulders and gave a short mirthless laugh. "I'm sorry, Susan. I'm talking like a clod. Naturally you are keen to get back to your own full life in London . . . your interests there . . . your work. It's just that I wasn't expecting it quite so soon and it was a bit of a shock." She saw his lips quiver. "It has been so good having you here . . . and Jan." His whole face softened as he spoke her name.

So that was it, Susan thought with a pang. It was Jan he wanted at Glenelg "for keeps," and he was too much in love to care how many barriers stood in the way. The conversation had brought him up with a jerk—making him realize that their visit to Glenelg was coming to an end.

For a long bleak moment she looked into his stormy

dark eyes, knowing the passion that burned in them was not for her—but for Jan.

"Have you told her what's in the wind?" he asked.

"No." Susan hesitated. "My mother's letter has only just arrived. I'm . . . afraid Jan won't like it very much. I'll keep it until after we have been to the hospital this afternoon I think. I'm going with her. . . ." she added.

"I'll drive you in," Iain said quickly.

Susan looked up sharply. "But you ought not to spare the time."

"I know I ought not to," he glowered at her. "But Jan has been getting wet all week in this wretched weather. The least I can do is to see that she makes her final trip to the hospital in comfort."

"Kirstie won't like it," Susan blurted.

"Let's leave Kirstie out of it if you don't mind!" Iain jumped to his feet with such force that his chair went spinning. He picked it up and set it noisily in place. "Don't you *want* me to come into Edinburgh with you this afternoon?"

"Of course, I want you. . . . " If only he knew how much!

"Then for heaven's sake stop arguing about it. I won't have very many more chances of driving you places . . . don't grudge me this last afternoon."

A last afternoon with Jan was what he meant, of course. In a brief electrical silence he looked down at her . . . uncertainly, pleadingly. It was as if he were begging her to understand.

CHAPTER TEN

THE RAIN CEASED as they set off. By the time they reached Edinburgh the sun was shining. "It's a good omen!" Jan exulted. Suddenly she was in one of her extravagantly hopeful moods again.

"I know exactly what I'm going to say to Tony," she declared as they went down the long green corridor. "It can't possibly fail! You'll see!"

Susan trembled for her groundless optimism.

On the landing of the men's surgical ward nurse awaited them. "Ah, Jan, there you are! I wanted to catch you before you went into the ward. And you've brought your sister with you, I see." She nodded approvingly at Susan. "It's just as well, in the circumstances. All sorts of things have been happening." She paused, looking a little uneasy. "Come into my office a moment," she suggested. "We can talk better there."

They followed her into the pleasant little room with its chintzes and flowers—oasis of homeliness in a clinical wilderness.

"Mr. Brampton is much better," the nurse began. She looked at Jan piercingly, as if trying to brace her for what was to come. "You remember I told you that he probably needed just the one sharp stimulus to set his memory in motion again? Well, he seems to have had just that. A visitor arrived for him from Moorings this morning—his fiancée.''

Jan who was standing by the desk put out a hand for support. "But that's . . . quite mad!" she said with a strained little laugh.

"A very charming girl," the nurse went on relentlessly, "a Miss Trent. She had read the account of Mr. Brampton's accident in the newspapers . . . and set off for Edinburgh as soon as she could. She is with him now."

Jan just stood there staring at her. Every shred of color drained from her cheeks.

"Perhaps you didn't know of their engagement," the nurse prompted gently. She turned to Susan. "It would have been a help if we had been told of it. We could have got in touch with Miss Trent earlier. . . ."

Susan said, "Yes, of course," in a bewildered way. Her brain was in a whirl, her whole concern for Jan. Of all the unexpected developments! It was like some crazy dream.

"There seems to have been a misunderstanding," she began helplessly. Jan's lips worked as if she were trying to speak. Susan put an arresting hand on her arm.

"No, Jan, don't say anything just now. Leave it until we've seen Sandra." It would be unbearable to hear her pouring out the story of her true relationship to Tony, only to have it discredited. Whatever had happened today Sandra Trent had apparently got the nurse wholly on her side—the nurse who all along had looked on Jan as a pushing little interloper taking advantage of the famous Mr. Brampton's mental blackout to stake her romantic, schoolgirlish claim.

The nurse glanced from one stricken face to the other. "Miss Trent tells me you are neighbors of hers at Moorings." There was reproach in her tone. Obviously she was convinced they had been keeping quiet about Sandra's existence for their own dubious reasons.

"I've spoken to her just once in my life," Susan said tersely. "Jan has had more to do with her—"

"I certainly have!" Jan burst in, with a mirthless laugh. "And I might have guessed she'd do something like this as soon as she read about Tony's accident in the papers. But if she thinks she's going to do herself any good coming here . . . telling lies. . . ." She shook off Susan's restraining hand, and rushed from the office.

"There must be no emotional scenes, Miss Harrowby!" the nurse called after her sharply. She turned to Susan with an outraged air. "All this is most irregular. Mr. Brampton is by no means out of the wood yet, and I can't have him worried. I wish now I'd refused your sister admission today . . . you'd better go along and see that she behaves sensibly. I'll give you five minutes," she warned.

"There's more in all this than I'm able to tell you, nurse," Susan explained breathlessly, and hurried after Jan.

They walked down the long ward in silence. Jan striding ahead, bristling with suppressed fury. The screens were still in place around Tony's bed—giving a semblance of privacy. Sandra, perched on the edge of the bed, stood up to greet them, momentarily blocking their view of Tony, propped on his pillows. She looked tall and opulent in a light elegant travel coat, her golden hair swathed thickly around her head in the latest fashion. Slender bangles jingled on her wrists as she held out her hand, with an affected, "Why Jan, and Susan . . . how nice to see you!"

Jan thrust her aside without ceremony and kneeling by the bed caught Tony's hands in her own. "Darling!" she began breathlessly, "The nurse tells me your memory has come back!"

"It has—more or less." He smiled into her eager uplifted face. "When Sandra, bless her, walked in on me today, the mists parted."

"Then you know who I am?"

Tony gently disengaged his hands. "Of course I do, my dear. Little Jan Harrowby, the most promising student at the Oakford Art School. I remember distinctly the excellent work you were doing. . . ."

Jan shrank back as though he had struck her. "But . . . that was only the beginning, Tony!"

"The beginning of what?" Sandra mocked with a confident smirk. She resumed her seat on the bed and turned blandly to Susan as though inviting her to share in her amusement. "The ward nurse tells me you and Jan have been marvelous, visiting Tony nearly every day since his accident. You came up to Edinburgh for the festival, I suppose?"

"No," Susan said, "we didn't." She glanced at the thin, vaguely troubled face on the pillows. "Maybe Tony could tell you why we came. . . ."

"I'm . . . afraid I haven't a clue!" Tony made a small defensive gesture.

"Then your memory *hasn't* returned," Jan said fiercely. She straightened up and leaned close to him. "Look at me, Tony," she commanded. "Look into my eyes!"

"Really!" Sandra mocked. "What is this? Hypnosis?"

Jan ignored her, desperately holding Tony's puzzled gaze. "We came up to Edinburgh together, darling," she urged. "We were going to be married."

Tony's lips twitched. Sandra laughed aloud. "Honestly, Jan, your imagination does you credit! Tony remembers perfectly well meeting you on the train . . . naturally you traveled together, he couldn't very well have cut you dead.''

"Is that what you told her, Tony?" Jan asked.

Tony passed a hand across his brow. "As far as I remember that's how it must have been. But it's all frightfully hazy . . . the whole Edinburgh trip, I mean. I suppose I must have decided to come and have a look at the festival. I know I wanted to see the art collection. But as for marrying anybody . . . ." The smile tugged again at his lips. "Well, there you've got me beat, honey!" He patted Jan's hand. "Don't look so stricken, my dear. You're a sweet child, and I can't think of anything nicer than eloping to Edinburgh with you, but I hardly flatter myself you'd be interested in an old wreck like me."

So that was the line he had decided to take—mild badinage. Jan stood up, her eyes glassy and fixed, her whole body quivering with outrage. "I just don't believe you, Tony. I can't. You either remember me or you don't. And you obviously *do* remember me. If you've changed toward me for some reason or other and want to break up everything that was between us . . . this is about the meanest possible way to do it."

There was an uneasy silence. Sandra jingled her bangles impatiently. Tony went a faint, shamed red.

"You know, I suppose," Jan shot at him, her voice rising shrilly, "that Sandra is passing herself off here as your fiancée?"

"I had to," Sandra put in hurriedly. "It was the only way I could persuade that old battle-ax of a nurse to let me into the ward this morning outside visiting hours. I've told Tony about it, of course. We've laughed over it. . . ."

Tony took her hand. "Sandra and I understand one another," he said quietly. "We are old friends." He looked up at her in frank adoration. "She has come like an angel of light to me today, giving me back my s-sanity. You don't know what a nightmare it has been lying here in this ghastly place, with only a shadowy inkling as to who I was, or why I was, or what it was all about."

"Poor lamb!" Sandra leaned over and dropped a light kiss on his forehead. "But the nightmare is over now, and I'm taking you home with me as soon a I can get the doctor to sign your discharge." She turned brightly to Susan. "The nurse thinks there is no reason whatever why Tony shouldn't travel south. I've got the most divinely comfortable car and we can take our time and do the journey in easy stages."

"It sounds too good to be true!" Tony sighed. He lifted Sandra's hand and pressed it to his lips. They gazed at one another in rapt content. Susan didn't dare to look at Jan. The whole thing was so incredible. The sheer crazy frustration of it made her want to scream. Mercifully at that moment, the nurse appeared.

"You know," she announced with sprightly officialdom, "we really aren't supposed to have more than two visitors at a time. . . ."

"We're just going," Jan declared stonily. How could she be so composed? "Goodbye, Tony," she said quietly. Sandra, she ignored. Murmuring ineffectual farewells, Susan followed her. She was aware of the nurse fluttering after them all the way down the green corridor, as if to make certain that they really left the premises. It was wonderful, wasn't it, she remarked with ghastly brightness, how much better Mr. Brampton was today. Miss Trent's visit had been a godsend!

At the main exit Jan turned to her. "Would you say Mr. Brampton has completely recovered from his amnesia?" she demanded.

"Well, yes!" the nurse agreed. "He doesn't remember his accident, of course, but that is to be expected. He probably never will remember it, which is one of the merciful things about extreme surgical shock."

"But there is no reason now why he shouldn't remember . . . everything else?"

"No reason at all."

"Thanks," Jan snapped. "That's all I wanted to know."

She went out into the courtyard and walked rapidly, blindly past Iain in the waiting station wagon.

"Jan!" Susan called after her. She swung around, her eyes black holes in her pale, tense face. Iain looked at her and then at Susan in concerned inquiry. "How did it go today?" he asked.

"Fine," Jan said hoarsely. "Just fine. Tony's memory has come back all in a rush and he has decided that I'm a clever little art student he used to know and that he is more or less engaged to a girl called Sandra Trent." She opened the door of the car and got in.

Iain turned to Susan in mystification. She said hurriedly, "A girl from Moorings has turned up . . . someone Tony was once keen on. He seems to think he still is." She climbed in beside Jan. Iain took his place in the driver's seat. He paused with his hand on the gear shift, eyeing Jan at his side uneasily.

"He'll snap out of it, Jan," he offered gently. "After all he has been through he is bound to be a bit confused."

"He isn't confused, just fiendishly clever," Jan said in a tight voice. "It all ties up with the way he has been acting for days . . . all that stuff about defense mechanisms—a convenient amnesia blotting out things that were too much for him. Maybe it was genuine at first, but he has realized now that he's onto a good thing, and he's sticking to it— anything to get himself out of the jam he is in, running away with a teenager.''

"Aren't you being a bit hard on the poor chap? Surely he'd tell you straight out if that's how he felt?" Iain suggested.

"You don't know anything about it," Jan cut him off rudely. "Anyway, it's nobody's business but mine. I'll be glad if you'll please not talk about it anymore."

"Sure!" Iain agreed curtly, nettled at the snub. "The sooner Mr. Tony Brampton and his tantrums are a closed book the better as far as I'm concerned."

"That makes two of us," Jan muttered, and shut her mouth like a clamp.

They drove on in uncomfortable silence. Never had the road to Glenelg seemed so long. Susan racked her brains for some comfort she might offer, but Jan was too raw with pain to bear even the gentlest touch. For days she had been living under intense strain, waiting for Tony's clouded mind to clear. Now he had come back to life . . . only to turn to Sandra Trent. It was a slight she would never forgive, and with characteristic impetuosity she had jumped to the conclusion that it was deliberate. Tony had jilted her. This was the end—final as the thrust of a knife. Perhaps it was better so . . . Susan thought, less harmful than the bitter quarrel with her father, which was the only alternative. The truth was that there had never been the remotest chance of a happy ending to her love for Tony Brampton. It wasn't Sandra Trent who had wrecked her romance, but her own childish status in law, making her subject to parental control. Would it help if this were pointed out to her? Mulling it over Susan saw they had reached the hazel-tree lane, and were running downhill to the bridge that spanned the singing burn.

"Will you put me down here?" Jan demanded. "I want to be by myself for a while . . . I'm going for a walk up the valley."

For a moment or two Iain made no attempt to drive on. Hunched over the wheel he gazed at Jan's retreating form. Walking slowly along the path by the noisy little burn, her head bent, her shoulders bowed, she looked forlorn and desolate.

"Hopes Valley," Iain said, "that has nothing to do with hope. Like lots of place names around here it is a legacy from the long ago days of the Norse invasions—a corruption of the word 'haup,' which means a dead end—the valley that leads nowhere . . ." he broke off with a bitter laugh. "Just the spot for a jolly little saunter with a vanishing dream." He started the car with an impatient jerk. "Just exactly what did happen to Jan at the hospital today?" he asked, as they drove through the gates of Glenelg.

Briefly, Susan told him.

He made a shocked, incredulous sound. "What a jolt for poor old Jan! Enter the not-so-dumb blonde! Do you think Brampton was genuinely taken in by her claims on him?"

"I don't know," Susan mused. "It's impossible to be certain. It seems a bit odd that if he remembers all about his life at Moorings—and he obviously does—that he should have so entirely forgotten his relationship to Jan. He was so much in love with her." She thought about it a moment and then went on. "He may, of course, have realized how hopeless it was to carry on with plans for a marriage my father will never permit. But it seems a pretty low way to wriggle out of it.''

"He could have decided to wait until Jan is twenty-one,'' Iain suggested.

Susan shook her head. "He's not the waiting sort . . . and four years is a heck of a long time.''

"It wouldn't be to me if I were in his shoes,'' Iain declared, and saw the sudden look of pain in Susan's gray eyes. "Poor Susan!'' He laid a light hand on her arm. "You're suffering over all this as much as Jan, aren't you?''

"Not quite,'' Susan said with a stifled sigh. "She must be going through sheer hell today, and much as I love her I can only look on . . . and sympathize, trying to imagine all that it means to her.''

"The pangs of unrequited love!'' Iain gave a sardonic laugh. "Not your line of country, is it, Susan? You're far too sensible and well balanced. When you fall in love it will all be orderly and well planned . . . like the files and records in my office. A place for everything, and everything in its right place—even your heart.''

She couldn't answer him, her throat suddenly constricting. Thankfully, she saw that they had reached the house.

Refusing to wait for tea, Iain rushed off to catch up on neglected chores. "He had no business to go in to Edinburgh this afternoon,'' Kirstie grumbled inevitably. "Worrying himself silly in case a few drops of rain fell on his precious Jan! He must have known perfectly well the weather was going to clear. There was every sign of it before lunch. Where is Jan, by the way?'' she asked as she put the teapot on the table. "Didn't you bring her back with you?''

"She has gone for a walk up the valley," Susan explained, and then, because it had to be done sooner or later, told Kirstie something of what had happened at the hospital. Kirstie listened in open-mouthed astonishment.

"That artist laddie seems to have a knack of tangling himself up with lovesick girls," she remarked dryly when Susan had done. "Jan is well rid of him. But I've had no opinion of him from the start. No right-minded man would take a girl of that age from her home against her parents' wishes."

Drinking a badly needed cup of tea, Susan reflected that life would be very simple if you were constituted like Kirstie—all the whites were so white and the blacks so black. And never for a moment did she doubt her own judgment.

"I suppose this will be the end of it now," she was saying on an odd note of regret. "There'll be nothing to keep you at Glenelg any longer."

"Our parents are driving up tomorrow to fetch us," Susan said. "I heard from mother this morning." She took the letter from her pocket and pushed it across the table. "Do read it," she urged, as Kirstie hesitated. "There are messages of gratitude in it for you . . . and Iain. I didn't have a chance to show it to you before, in the rush of getting off to the hospital."

Kirstie took the folded sheet from the envelope and scanned it hurriedly. "She's o'er kind to me," she murmured as she read Mrs. Harrowby's glowing words of gratitude. "It's been a pleasure having you."

With a preoccupied air she refilled their teacups and pressed Susan to have another scone. They were eating at the gate-legged table in the kitchen window; Tibby, the cat, in his customary place among the geraniums on the sill waited hopefully for his saucer of milk. Savoring the homely scene Susan felt a pang of almost unbearable nostalgia. It seemed incredible that in a matter of hours, she must leave it all behind.

"I shall miss you," Kirstie burst out suddenly, feelingly.

"And I shall miss you," Susan murmured inadequately.

"We've got along fine," Kirstie went on with a catch in her voice. "You've been a great help to me, Susan . . . and it's not only your work about the house I'm meaning." There was a look of desolation in her fine hazel eyes—Iain's eyes, her one beautiful feature.

"Whiles, it's lonesome here, and I'm not much of a one for making friends," she confessed. "But the moment I saw you I took a liking to you. We could be happy together running this house . . . we make a good team." She folded a buttered drop scone and bit into it savagely. "Why couldn't it have been you instead of Jan that caught Iain's fancy?"

Susan went a sudden bright scarlet. "Really, Kirstie!"

"I'm sorry," Kirstie apologized. "I had no right to say that." She gave a small embarrassed laugh. "As if you had nothing better to do than sit here waiting for Iain to ask you to marry him! You'll have plenty of men in London to choose from I'll be bound!"

"Well, of course!" Susan laughed, with some vague notion of restoring her injured dignity. The remark about Iain's preference for Jan rankled ridiculously.

"And one special man, maybe?" Kirstie probed.

Susan put a finger to her lips mysteriously. "That would be telling!"

"Oh, well," Kirstie sighed regretfully. "I might have guessed. But it would have been a bonny thing for me if it had . . . been otherwise. Whiles, I fret myself, wondering what sort of girl Iain will choose for a wife. It will make a big difference to me, when the time comes, having to live with another woman in the house—and that woman the mistress of the place." She paused an instant and then added a little unsteadily, "It would have been all right with you, Susan. It would have been fine."

Moved by this tribute, nervous of showing how deeply disturbing she found the whole conversation, Susan remained silent.

Getting up from the table Kirstie busied herself giving Tibby his saucer of milk, and when she spoke again it was to wonder if there was any point in keeping the kettle on the boil for Jan.

"I wouldn't bother," Susan advised. "In her present mood she'll not be worrying over missing her tea. She'll probably walk for hours, poor kid. Trying to outpace her heartache. I don't suppose she'll be back much before supper."

But suppertime came around and no Jan appeared. Iain sat through the meal in uneasy silence. "Do you think she may have lost her way?" he burst out at last.

Kirstie gave him a withering glance. "In broad daylight? Even if she did go astray she'd only got to climb the nearest bit of high ground and look around her. Glenelg with its white walls stands out for miles."

"All the same, if she doesn't show up soon I'm going out to look for her," Iain persisted.

"And who's to load the van for the morning?" Kirstie inquired frostily.

It was most embarrassing. With a twinge of impatience for the absent Jan, Susan said hurriedly, "She'll be all right, Iain. She'll just have gone farther than she meant to, I expect."

"And she'll come home when it suits her," Kirstie snapped. "Her sort always does."

Susan colored. Whatever Kirstie might feel about herself, she'd be thankful to see the last of Jan—with her disruptive influence on Iain's work.

Pushing his plate of apple pie aside almost untouched, Iain stalked off to see to the vegetable packing. Susan began to clear the table.

"Leaving his good pudding!" Kirstie growled, scraping the spurned apple pie into the bin of scraps she kept for the hens. Then, as if to make amends for her ill temper, she announced she would put a match to the drawing-room fire and they could have a cosy evening. "I can't believe it is to be almost your last!" she sighed as they settled down to listen to the battery operated radio.

Uneasily, Susan watched the dusk deepening beyond the long elegant windows. Surely Jan ought to be back by now! Iain came in just as the nine o'clock news was starting. He swept the shadowy firelit room with a piercing glance. "Hasn't Jan turned up yet?" he demanded sharply.

"No," Susan said in a small voice. "I'm beginning to be a bit worried."

Kirstie put down her knitting. "Maybe you'd better go look for her after all, Iain," she suggested, with unexpected meekness. Her capitulation put the final touch to Susan's rising panic.

"Not that she'll have got far if she went up the valley," Kirstie went on, as if trying to allay some unspoken fear. "There's naught there but the reservoir . . . and no road beyond it."

"The reservoir!" Susan echoed, and all the color drained from her face.

Iain stared at her, his eyes dilating. "My God!" he

whispered hoarsely. "The reservoir! You don't think . . .!"

"I don't think anything," Susan all but shrieked at him. "But we've got to find Jan . . . and bring her home . . . right away!"

"Go and get your coat," Iain ordered grimly. "I'll fetch a lantern from the stables . . . and a length of rope."

CHAPTER ELEVEN

OUT OF DOORS the twilight still lingered, but in the valley the shadows were long and the water of the burn held a steely coldness. Sheep grazing the slopes of enclosing land called to their lambs. Their cries echoing plaintively on the darkening air filled Susan with a sense of utter desolation.

She had to run to keep up with Iain's rapid strides. He seemed unaware of her, forging ahead, driven by the same dark fear that made her own heart falter. The way was endless. Breathlessly she stumbled on. In nightmare dreams as long as she lived she would find herself running down this interminable valley, seeing its every detail in hideous clarity, its beauty distorted by terror.

When they came to a five-barred gate that blocked their path, Iain vaulted it lightly and stood on the other side, waiting for her. She clambered up to the top rail and halted there, looking down at him. They had not once spoken in their urgent haste, but now in the swift glance exchanged they read each other's inarticulate dread.

"Don't, Susan!" Iain begged in a low troubled tone. "Don't look like that, darling. We'll find Jan, never fear!" He held out his arms to her and blindly she let herself drop into them. For a timeless moment he held her against his heart. She could hear its turbulent beating as he poured out half-incoherent words of comfort, pressing her face against his rough tweed shoulder and stroking her hair, as if he were reassuring a frightened child. It could be nothing more, she told herself, even as the wild, unbidden rapture flooded her heart. Not love, but compassion held her close. Yet it helped—that brief physical contact, like life pouring into her veins giving her fresh courage.

When they set off again he took her hand, steadying her over the rough places, guiding her through the deepening night. The valley had widened now to a grassy clearing, dotted around with white-painted skeps murmurous with late homing bees. Rosebay willow herb stood shoulder high in the rank grass. Tall plumes of meadow sweet burned like pale flames in the dusk, filling the air with their heady sweetness. They had come to the end of the path, Susan saw. A soaring grassy embankment blocked their way—the reservoir. As they climbed the steep escarpment, her heart hammered painfully. There was a paved walk at the top, flanked by a breast-high parapet of stone. Looking over it, they could see the vast sheet of water far below, girt around with the blocks of granite that had once enclosed Calton Jail. Here and there the water lapped against small pebbly beaches, strewn with boulders of the roughly hewn stone. It was a scene of utter loneliness under the high, cold sky. The lost-soul call of a curlew made Susan cover her eyes with her hands. "Where do we begin to look now?" she murmured brokenly.

"God knows!" Iain answered between clenched teeth. "She could have climbed down to the water's edge. . . ."

Or flung herself down, Susan thought with a shudder.

Iain cupped his hands to his mouth and sent out a long "Hel . . . lo!" It echoed forlornly against the stones, so that the small answering call was at first almost lost to them. When they heard it clearly the second time Susan clutched Iain's arm. "She answered, Iain . . . somebody answered!"

"Jan!" she yelled frenziedly. "Jan! Where are you?"

They saw her then, a small dark figure climbing over the tumbled boulders, coming toward them. The relief was so great that Susan found herself half sobbing, half laughing.

"Oh, Jan," she called, running to meet her. "You've given us such a fright. You've been gone more than five hours. We were so worried. . . ."

"I'd no idea it was so late," Jan returned with an assumption of carelessness. But her face in the dim light had a drugged look, her eyes shadowy and sunken, her nostrils pinched as though with actual physical pain. She turned to Iain with a pitiful attempt at a laugh. "What on earth did you think had happened to me? Were you going to drag the reservoir with that . . . ?" She pointed in derision to the rope he carried.

"We thought you might have had an accident," Iain offered lamely.

She shook her head, still keeping up the jaunty pose. "No you didn't. You thought I had come here to . . . end it all—in the grand manner. But you needn't have worried. I wouldn't give Sandra Trent the satisfaction of gloating over my watery grave." Her voice rose hysterically. With a visible effort she steadied herself. "Actually I was sitting down there in a sheltered corner, basking in the sun as long as it lasted . . . making notes for a new painting."

Susan gave it up with a shaken laugh. The last thing she had expected was to find Jan interesting herself in a painting project! Artists, perhaps, had reserves to draw on unknown to more ordinary mortals. "Jan, you're wonderful!" she exclaimed.

"What's so wonderful about me?" Jan shrugged. "I

just got a hunch about all those terrible stones, that's all. They kept forming themselves into the most extraordinary patterns . . . as if they had a life of their own, menacing and cruel. If I can only remember it all . . . get it onto canvas . . . !''

"You will, Jan," Iain humored her. "But you're shaking with cold right now, and we ought to be making tracks for home." He put an arm around her shoulders and urged her gently along the paved way toward the embankment. They made the steep descent in silence, concentrating on keeping a foothold on the slippery, dew-wet grass. When they came to the flowery hollow, the late bees still droned around the doors of the hives, a sound that accentuated the eerie quietness. In the gathering darkness trees and grass were drained of all color. Shadowy shapes loomed. Somewhere a sheep coughed hollowly. Susan's taut nerves snapped.

"What was that?" she cried in alarm.

"An asthmatic goblin waiting to leap at you out of the bushes," Iain chaffed. They all laughed—not very convincingly. It wasn't a particularly convincing joke. But anything was better than plodding along in that dreadful strained silence.

"Thank goodness there weren't any asthmatic goblins down by the reservoir," Jan said. "But I'm glad you came to meet me. I'd have been scared to death if I'd had to walk back through this valley in the dark all on my lonesome."

Her flippant tone didn't deceive Susan in the least. Sooner or later the poor little facade of jauntiness would collapse—and the sooner the better. This rigid control was dangerous—and most unlike the impetuous, emotional Jan. Had she kept it up even while she was alone? Just what had been happening to her since she left them to walk down the valley path at four o'clock this afternoon?

"It must be quite a picture you have been painting," Susan probed.

"It's terrific!" Jan declared. "Just stones . . . and stones. A great gray wall rising up at the end of a valley called Hope." She gave a shrill little laugh. "Funny, isn't it? Quite a poetic parable—a path in the sunshine, leading you by the singing water, past the flowers and hives of honey . . . to a dead end. That's really the name of this valley . . . did you know? The Dead End!" She caught her breath in a great tearing sob.

"Hold it, Jan!" Iain said gently.

But the sobs came thick and fast now and her feet caught in the tangled grass. He put out his hands to steady her. She clutched at the lapels of his jacket, burying her face against his shoulder. "Oh, Iain, I can't bear it! I can't bear it! I don't want to go back to the house. I don't want to go anywhere . . . let me stay here. Just . . . leave . . . me!" The last words were a wail of despair.

"Would it help if I stayed with you, dear?" Iain asked softly.

Jan gave a long shivering sigh of acquiescence and burrowed into his shoulder like a tired child. He looked at Susan over the dark bowed head. "Maybe you'd better go on without us," he said. "Tell Kirstie we'll be along soon."

Susan swallowed a hard lump in her throat as she nodded agreement. It didn't occur to him to wonder if she could find her way, if she would be nervous walking by herself through the valley. He wanted to be alone with Jan—that was all that mattered to him. Hurrying along the river path, faintly illuminated now by the rising moon, Susan fought down the jealousy that gnawed at her heart. How could she think of herself at such a time? It was natural for Iain to want to stay with Jan, answering her desperate cry for help. In his love for her he could comfort her as no one else could. Instinctively, she had turned to him.

Half-blind with tears, Susan stumbled on. When she came to the five-barred gate she rested against it, remembering how Iain had held her in his arms, calling her "darling," giving her pity . . . brotherly affection . . . everything but the love she wanted from him—that miracle of recognition that would single her out from everyone else in the world as the one person he needed to make his life complete. But it would never happen. His heart had gone to Jan . . . who thought of him only as a refuge in her trouble. Later perhaps she might realize how much more he could be. She would teach him to speak her own language. It would not be hard. With his sensitive appreciation of music, his love of those formal beautiful Scottish dances, at which he excelled—he would understand her preoccupation with color and design. There was an artistic streak in Iain, and Jan would encourage it. Perhaps that was why she attracted him so strongly. If they married they would have a rich companionship. Crushing down her pain, Susan forced herself to face it. It seemed to her that it could all so easily come about. And it would be the perfect solution, saving Jan from the disillusionment of her broken romance. A heart caught on the rebound—not for the first time in history!

She has only to turn to him to find everything Tony has cheated her of, Susan thought bitterly. *And I think, in a way, she already knows it.*

Kirstie was at the gate of Glenelg, peering anxiously into

the gathering gloom, listening for their returning footsteps. "Have you found Jan?" she called out.

"She was sitting down by the reservoir, lost to all sense of time," Susan told her. "Iain will be bringing her home presently. . . ."

"Humph!" Kirstie grunted, none too pleased. "I suppose she hadn't a thought to spare for the anxiety she had caused us."

"She's . . . very upset," Susan offered feebly.

"But she'll console herself weeping on Iain's shoulder, I've no doubt!" Kirstie snapped.

They walked up the driveway in a rather uncomfortable silence. Lamplight streamed from the open hall door, and as they mounted the portico steps the telephone started ringing. Kirstie ran in to answer it, and with a brief, "Just a moment please. She's here!" handed the receiver to Susan.

It was her father speaking. They had made better time than they expected on their journey north and were already in Edinburgh. "We're putting up at the Waverley for the night," Dr. Harrowby said. "But we'll be out at Glenelg first thing in the morning." He was anxious to start the homeward journey without delay. "I hope there'll be no nonsense from Jan about coming along with us," he ended grimly.

"I think she'll be glad enough to get away," Susan told him, and left it at that. She couldn't go into the whole complicated story of Tony's strange defection on the phone.

It had been a good trip up, Dr. Harrowby went on. With a motorist's enthusiasm he talked for a few minutes about the roads, scenery and hotels they had encountered on the way. "I'm sorry we can't stay a little longer in these parts and get to know these kind friends of yours," he concluded. "But Heathershaw, who is doing duty for me, can't spare more than a few days from his own practice. As it is I'm indebted to Jan for the only break I'm likely to get this year." He laughed lightheartedly, accepting without question Susan's implication that the foolish elopement episode had fizzled out. How maddeningly complacent and unimaginative the best of men could sometimes be!

Susan hung up the receiver with a heavy heart. "The parents are in Edinburgh, " she told the hovering Kirstie. "They will be coming to take us home tomorrow. . . ."

"Ay-ee, I'm sorry!" Kirstie burst out spontaneously. She caught Susan's hand in her own. "But it'll not be 'goodbye.' You'll come back, won't you, Susan? Any time you feel in need of a breath of good Scottish fresh air, there'll be a welcome waiting on you at Glenelg. You'll remember that, now?"

"You're a darling, Kirstie. I'll remember!" Bending forward Susan dropped a quick kiss on Kirstie's thin cheek. As she ran up the stairs there were tears again on her lashes. *I'm turning into a regular waterspout,* she told herself impatiently, as she groped on her bedside table for candle and matches. On the chest of drawers the big oil lamp, with the globe like a creamy full moon, stood ready to light. She must start packing. If she knew anything about her father he would be out at Glenelg right after breakfast . . . and he hated being kept waiting, especially when he was setting out on a long drive.

As she folded her few garments away in her suitcase she listened to the familiar sounds of the old house: the grandfather clock ticking ponderously on the staircase landing; the distant rattle of fire irons that indicated Kirstie was banking down the kitchen stove for the night. Beyond the open window the country quietness whispered—that stillness soft as breathing, as full of life as the gentle beating of a heart at peace. She could hear the secret rustle of the sleeping trees, the far-off hooting of an owl; in some distant farm a cow lowed mournfully. This time next week Susan reflected bleakly, she'd be back in her Cromwell Gardens apartment, listening to the never ceasing roar of the London traffic.

It was late when Jan came up to bed. Kirstie had insisted upon her having a meal when she got in. "She gave me tea and scrambled eggs, and a lecture on the error of my ways," Jan said with a shrug. "Though she didn't actually say so, I could see she didn't approve of my nocturnal stroll with Iain. Funny old Kirstie . . . it's so like her to stay up till all hours to cook a meal, and then scold you while you are eating it."

Susan, eyeing her anxiously, saw that the air of intolerable strain had gone, though her eyes were suspiciously red, and she looked very weary. But her calm wasn't forced or unnatural anymore. Her hour with Iain had steadied her . . . given her some kind of comfort. Just what had they said to one another as they walked home through the moonlit valley? Susan couldn't help wondering. Sharply, she turned away from the thought. She had to tell Jan that their parents were already in Edinburgh, and she hadn't even known they were on their way. Would the news of their arrival be a shock to her? It was a relief to discover that Iain had prepared her.

"He told me they would probably be here by tomorrow evening," Jan said quietly. "Having decided, I suppose, to rush up and rescue me once and for all from Tony Brampton's fell clutches! If only they had known how things are, they needn't have bothered." It was just a little too flippant to be convincing, but she spoke Tony's name without any visible sign of emotion.

"They've arrived already," Susan announced. "I had a phone call from dad just after I got in this evening. They are sleeping at the Waverley Hotel tonight and will be out here first thing in the morning. We have to start off for Moorings right away. Dad is anxious to get back."

Jan looked a little startled, but all she said was, "I'd better get cracking and pack my things then."

It wasn't until long after they had got to bed that she spoke again of her walk with Iain. For an hour Susan had lain by her side, waiting for the sounds of gentle breathing that would tell her Jan had gone to sleep . . . half-dreading to hear instead the telltale sniff of smothered weeping. When the grandfather clock on the stairs struck midnight, Susan felt her turn cautiously and grope for the glass of water she invariably kept on her bedside table.

"Can't you sleep, Jan?" she whispered.

"I never in my life felt more wide-awake," Jan confessed. "It has been one hell of a day, hasn't it? I feel as if I'd lived about a hundred years . . . and was that much older." There was an ominous quiver in her voice and it was a moment before she spoke again. Flinging herself back on her pillows, she stretched her arms above her head. "Listen, Sue," she urged, "I want you to do something for me. Take mother and dad aside when they get here tomorrow, and ask them will they please not mention Tony to me ever again. You tell them what you like about what happened today, but they're not to try to make me talk about it. I don't want Tony's name mentioned in my presence . . . ever again as long as I live. Will you make that clear to them, Sue?"

"Of course, I will, darling," Susan agreed, a little tremulously.

Jan gave a long, quivering sigh. "If it wasn't for Iain I don't think I'd have had the courage to face them tomorrow. I had a wild idea of running away and getting a job . . . hiding myself somewhere. But Iain made me see that would be cowardly, and that the more you try to run away from things the more they hurt you in the end. I'd have to go back to Moorings sometime. It might as well be now. Even if I have to see Tony marching around the village with Sandra Trent." She drew in a convulsive breath. "It won't be *my* Tony. That Tony is dead. Perhaps he never existed, excepting in my imagination. . . ."

"Darling!" Susan said brokenly. "If only there was something I could do to help."

"There is," Jan burst out fiercely. "Just stop pitying me. I can't stand it. It is the last indignity." There was a moment of throbbing silence, then she went on more quietly, "That is what is so wonderful about Iain. He can be sorry for you without making you feel a worm. He even said I was to be envied because I'm a creative artist, with an artist's capacity for suffering, and that suffering can enrich my work."

"I knew he would be understanding," Susan offered humbly out of the darkness of the big curtained bed.

"I began to see myself as a second Van Gogh," Jan laughed at her own presumption. "I started to tell him about the nightmare picture I was going to make out of those stones—all bitter and hard and horrible. And then . . . I cried in his arms for a while. He said, 'Even stones have beauty, Jan . . . Don't forget they can build sanctuaries as well as prisons.' And I began to remember the way the colors came and went on the reservoir walls as I watched them

all through the long, long hours of the endless afternoon.
Like water reflecting the changing light. As the sun set they
seemed to hold every color of the rainbow . . . and suddenly,
as I talked to Iain, I knew that was the way my picture was
going to be. Not a valley of despair leading to a dead end,
but a path cut off by a barrier that blossoms in strange
beauty—a rainbow of stone. I can hardly wait to get home
to start on it!''

How clever Iain had been! How brilliantly intuitive.
Was it love that had given him the wisdom to guide Jan's
thoughts and emotions back to her painting? He couldn't
have hit on a more effective balm for her wounded spirit.
There was nothing but gratitude in Susan's heart as she
said, ''I'm so glad you've found a friend in Iain, Jan dear.
The only pity is that we live so far away from him. He'll
want to see that painting, won't he?''

''Oh, but he's going to see it.'' There was a new
eagerness in Jan's voice now. ''He'll be coming to London
at the end of October to attend an agricultural show, and
I've asked him to Moorings for a weekend. Meanwhile, I'll
be writing to him to let him know how the picture is pro-
gressing.''

So it wouldn't be a final ''goodbye'' tomorrow, Susan
thought with a crazy sense of reprieve. She would see Iain
again in October . . . when he came to claim Jan. She would
be ready and waiting for him by then . . . free of her last
regrets for Tony.

CHAPTER TWELVE

ON A crisp autumn morning some weeks later Susan put the cover on her typewriter, locked up her desk, and ran down the dusty staircase of Digby Timber Imports Ltd. to join the home-going throng. It was Saturday, midday, and she was off to Moorings for the weekend. As she fought her way onto a crowded bus, Glenelg seemed very far away. It was amazing—and a little disconcerting—how easily she had slipped back into the old routine. Her work, her apartment, her various clubs, the evenings at concerts and theaters . . . and buried away under it all the memory of an old white house among the Lowland hills. Only at nights, in the drifting dreams between sleeping and waking would she allow herself to think of it, with a homesick yearning. As if she had spent half her lifetime within its sturdy walls, instead of a brief three weeks. But love is not measurable by time. The nagging pain in her heart was so much a part of her now that she seldom acknowledged it. What couldn't be cured must be endured, and Susan was good at enduring. More than one male glance that sunny morning lingered on her strong, serene face with its level brows and clear gray eyes. There was a sweet maturity about her, a poise and winsomeness of which she was wholly unaware. The quiet assurance that comes of hard-won selflessness.

At Victoria Station she bought an early edition of an

evening paper. As the train rocketed noisily through the suburbs she turned the pages, idly at first and then with a quickening of interest. The gossip page carried a photograph of Sandra Trent and a paragraph announcing her imminent marriage to "fashionable portraitist, Anthony Brampton." There were fulsome allusions to Sandra's beauty, her socialite activities, and a description of the historic manor that her wealthy financier father had recently purchased near Oakford in Sussex.

The news of the wedding wasn't altogether unexpected. But Susan wondered how Jan would take it. Since their return from Scotland she had seemed wholly absorbed in her studies at the art school. A rather more subdued Jan than of old, given to keeping her own council, though she would sometimes share parts of Iain's letters with Susan when she was at home for a weekend. They came pretty regularly, those well-filled envelopes with the Elginbridge postmark. Did they mean as much to Jan as Iain must have hoped they did? It was impossible to tell. She never spoke of Tony. His convalescence at Morrings Manor had been a long one, and the villagers, scenting romance, had kept the grapevine busy with details of his progress; and of Sandra's devotion. There were several versions of his accident in Edinburgh and of the dramatic loss of memory—from which Sandra had rescued him.

By some miracle, for which the Harrowbys couldn't be too thankful, Jan's runaway journey with Tony had eluded the wagging tongues, and even Sandra seemed to have decided to keep quiet about it. Perhaps because it was an episode difficult to admit without acknowledging the fact that Tony had at one time been more than ordinarily interested in Jan. Why else would they have gone off together to Edinburgh? The whole situation indeed bristled with humiliating pointers, awkward to explain away. So the less said about it, the better. That, no doubt, was how Sandra's mind had worked, Susan concluded. And now she had got Tony just where she wanted him—practically at the altar steps.

Did the family know of the impending marriage, Susan wondered, as she hurried up the familiar garden path. Tucking the evening paper into her holdall, she decided to wait and see. References to Tony Brampton were still liable to disturb the domestic peace, especially with her father, so it would be best to say nothing, unless the subject was brought up.

The house held an afternoon somnolence as she opened the unlatched hall door. Lunch would have been over an hour ago. She was always late for it when she came home on this midday train. There was a note from her mother on the hall table, telling her cold tongue, salad and fruit had been left for her in the fridge. "I've had to go to the British Legion Rummage Sale at the institute," Mrs. Harrowby wrote. "But I'll be back in time for tea. You'll find Jan painting in her studio." It was an old summerhouse at the end of the back garden that she had rigged up as a work-room since her return from Edinburgh.

Susan carried her food into the dining room, where a place at the table had been left for her. Feeling a little flat and neglected she ate without much zest. She had forgotten her mother would be out, though the legion rummage sale was an annual event of which she was the chief organizer, and invariably took place on this particular Saturday. The house seemed strangely lifeless without her. *No matter how grown-up you may think you are*, Susan reflected, *coming home means finding mother!*

She was clearing the table when her father came in. He

had been out on an emergency call, he explained, and in answer to Susan's inquiry, said he had had lunch before he went out. "Can't you leave that for a moment?" he asked a little impatiently, as he watched her stacking the dishes on a tray. "There's something I want to talk to you about, Susan," he went on with an oddly urgent air. "Let's go over to the office."

Feeling vaguely uneasy, she followed him into the annex that housed waiting room, consulting room and the tiny sterilizing room with a surgical couch that was used for examinations and minor operations: all very clean and bare and clinical, smelling faintly of drugs and disinfectant. A garden door in the waiting room made it possible for patients to walk straight in without approaching the residential part of the house.

They went into the consulting room, and the doctor seated himself at his desk, waving Susan to the chair set in front of it. "Young Brampton came to see me yesterday," he announced, without any preamble.

Susan drew in a sharp breath. "Tony Brampton came *here*?"

Dr. Harrowby nodded, looking mildly gratified at the sensation he had caused. "Marched in in the middle of evening office hours, as cool as you please, and said he'd come to consult me about his mental condition. Quite obviously he hadn't the slightest recollection of ever having seen me before . . . introduced himself, apologized for barging in without any medical card or introduction, but said he was desperately in need of help."

"What . . . kind of help?" Susan asked in a small, dazed voice. It was all so unexpected she couldn't quite take it in.

"It seems he hasn't been sleeping well recently." The doctor's tone became briskly professional, "I asked him why he didn't contact the London specialist who attended him after the accident, and he said he couldn't very well do that without the Trents finding out. He specially didn't want Sandra to know he had come to me . . . since she seems to be at the root of the trouble. She had been very devoted, nursing him back to health all these weeks, he said, but now she seems to expect him to marry her, and he is not sure of his feelings for her. The gap in his memory worries him; he still can't remember why he went to Edinburgh. He's got an idea there was a reason of extreme and vital importance behind the journey. It nags at him, just beyond the threshold of consciousness, haunting him in dreams . . . from which he wakes in a state of great distress.''

''He wasn't just pretending to have forgotten eloping with Jan, then?'' Susan put in.

The doctor's eyebrows shot up. ''Was that what you thought? Oh, no, he has forgotten it genuinely enough, and as far as I'm concerned, I wish he would go on forgetting it! But it is making him nervously ill.'' He gave Susan an anguished glance. ''It is putting me in a hell of a spot, Sue! As a father, I could wish Brampton the other end of the earth . . . but as a doctor, I'm committed to helping him.''

''And do you think you can?'' Susan asked, half-aghast at the possibility and its implications.

''Not personally. Nervous disorders are not my province. But there's a neurologist friend of mine in Harley Street to whom I can send him—chap called Stoke-Branden, first-rate at his job. I promised Brampton I'd phone S.B. and try to get him an early appointment. He's coming in this afternoon to find out what I've been able to fix up. Stoke-Branden will see him on Monday.''

"You mean Tony is coming here again today?" Susan repeated incredulously. "Does Jan know anything of this?"

"No, and there doesn't seem much point in telling her. It will only upset her all over again. And yet . . . I don't know. . . ." He paused uncertainly. "I rather wanted your view on it, Susan."

Susan could hardly believe her ears. Hitherto there had been only one view on this matter! Was her father beginning to relent in his attitude toward Tony Brampton? Or at least have doubts about its wisdom?

"I'm not happy about Jan," he went on in a troubled tone. "She has changed since she came back from Edinburgh. Goes about her work in a dogged sort of way, is obedient, docile . . . too docile. I miss the tantrums, the fireworks and enthusiasms." He picked up a pencil and stabbed savagely at a prescription pad. "There's no sparkle in her anymore—the life has gone out of her."

"What about her friendship with Iain MacDowell?" Susan put in a little breathlessly. "She writes to him frequently, doesn't she?"

The doctor shrugged. "I don't think there's very much in that. I wish there were! He's a sound chap—I like what I saw of him enormously, but he didn't strike me as Jan's cup of tea." He flung the pencil aside, as if dismissing Iain from the picture. "What bothers me most is . . . her attitude toward myself. You know how close to one another we were, Sue?" He looked at her hollowly. "Now she speaks to me only when she has to—shuts up like a clam when I come into the room and avoids me as much as possible. I've lost her, Susan." The words came out thickly, painfully. "Far more completely and tragically than if she had married and left us in the ordinary way."

There was a short, distressed silence. Susan's thoughts whirled. Everything had been so settled in her mind: Tony tied up with Sandra, Jan consoling herself with Iain—all the violent emotions of the summer, including her own, put tidily away. And now with a few words her father had wrecked the pattern. She looked at his haggard face with pity.

"Jan has been pretty badly hurt, dad," she said, "and it will take her a little while to get over it. But she will if you give her time."

He made a small gesture of despair. "I'm not so sure, Sue. She's an odd girl, passionate, tenacious, curiously mature for her years . . . and this thing about Brampton went very deep." He picked up the pencil and "doodled" mournfully. "There are times when I feel I'd give anything to see her her old happy self again. . . ."

It was just at that moment they heard the faint "ping" of the waiting-room bell. Someone had come in by the garden door.

"That will be Brampton," the doctor said jumping up from the desk. "Don't go!" he threw over his shoulder at Susan as he moved to open the consulting room door. "Come in, Mr. Brampton," he ordered brusquely.

Tony strode in with a breezy, "Good afternoon, doctor." Perhaps it was the beard, once more restored, that made him appear so confident and self-assured. In his thick, belted winter overcoat he seemed larger and more vital than Susan had remembered, and there was an air of well-being about him that didn't fit in with the story of his nervous distress. "Hello, Miss Harrowby!" he greeted her easily. "How nice to see you again!"

"You've met before, of course," the doctor recalled.

"In the Scottish mists!" Tony laughed. "Miss Harrowby

was kind enough to visit me in the hospital . . . when the mists were at their thickest. I hadn't a clue to her identity at the time—and only a cloudy idea of my own. I'm afraid I wasn't a very responsive invalid, but in my confused way I *was* grateful." He gave Susan a warm, quick smile. "Now that the confusion has gone. . . ."

"Are you telling us that the last distressing remnants of your amnesia have cleared up?" Dr. Harrowby broke in sharply.

"Just that, sir. Look!" He leaned across the desk, and lifting a lock of hair revealed a small egg-shaped lump on his forehead. "You don't have to make that Harley Street appointment for me after all. I'm my own man again . . . with mind and memory in focus and all the gaps filled in. It seems that all I was waiting for was another bang on the cranium."

The doctor's face was a study in conflicting emotions, professional interest struggling with resentment and apprehension.

"Extraordinary!" he murmured grimly. "But I have heard of similar cases." He rose and prodded at Tony's brow in clinical fascination. "Just how did it happen?" he asked.

Tony chuckled. "Our dear Miss Trent threw a heavy crystal paper weight at me—with murderous intent. Fortunately it didn't hit me squarely—just glanced off and landed harmlessly on one of Mrs. Trent's nice fat settee cushions. We were having one hell of a row, Sandra and I! It was when I got back to the manor last evening, just after my visit to you. I'd found Sandra in the hall at the telephone, giving an interview to some gossip hound on a London newspaper. She had, she informed me calmly, told him we were going to be married at an early date. I was

furious . . . naturally. Nothing of the kind had been
decided—as I told you yesterday. So—" he beamed
around at them both "—we had words. I'm not the type to
be caught by old tricks of that sort, and I told Sandra so
plainly. Whereupon she picked up the paperweight and
lammed it at me with all the force she could muster. I'm
not very clear as to what happened next. I must have
blacked out for a few moments. When I came to, I was sitting on the settee with my head in my hands . . . and the
mists and confusion had gone!" He dropped his air of
jauntiness and looked at the doctor gravely, almost
pleadingly. "It was a bit of a shock at first, as you can
imagine, and it took me a while to piece everything
together. But it was all there—quite clearly—my relationship with Jan, our elopement to Edinburgh . . . the blank
following my accident." He paused. "It began to dawn on
me, sir how . . . awkward for you my visit must have been
yesterday."

There was a short throbbing silence. Then Susan, who
could contain herself no longer, burst out, "I'm so glad,
Tony! I can't tell you how glad!"

The two men stared at her, as if they had forgotten her
existence.

"What are you going to do now?" Dr. Harrowby asked
Tony in a tight, strained voice.

Tony traced a pattern on the desk with a tentative forefinger. "Get my affairs in order . . . if it isn't too late!" He
lifted his head and gave the doctor a hard straight look.
"For a start, I've left the manor and gone back to my old
room at the Amberhurst Arms. Sandra is out of the picture
for good. From first to last she has played it crookedly.
How she could have had the gall to follow me to Edinburgh and persuade me I was more or less engaged to her, I

don't know! One thing my restored memory brought back to me was the fact that she was one of the few people who knew I intended to marry Jan. I had been forced to tell her, in order to disabuse her of certain romantic notions she was harboring." He broke off with a faintly embarrassed shrug. "So—there it is! I'm free and able to pick up my life again, and—with your permission, sir, I'd like to make my peace with Jan."

There was an ominous pause. Susan waited, with breath held back, her gaze fixed imploringly on her father's face. Never had he appeared more implacable. She watched his mouth tighten, saw the veins on his forehead swell. It seemed an interminable time before, at last, he turned to her. "Will you fetch Jan, my dear?" he said quietly, and she saw that there were tears in his eyes.

Blindly she hurried from the room, stunned by the immensity of the moment. Her father had given in—wholly and without reservation. There was no mistaking the quiet and deliberate capitulation. The resurrected Tony had been too much for him! Running through the deserted house and out into the back garden, Susan wondered how she was going to break the news to Jan. And what now of Iain? Her thoughts shied away from the question with something like panic. As she crossed the lawn, she was vaguely aware that the grass was crisp under her feet, with the first frost of winter. But it wasn't the cold that made her shiver.

The summerhouse door stood open, and she could see Jan in a paint-stained smock, putting her things away for the night. At the sound of Susan's approaching footsteps, she turned, her face lighting up in welcome.

"I was hoping you'd be out before it got quite dark," she said. "Come and look at my Hopes Valley picture. I've just finished it."

Susan gazed absently at the canvas on the large easel set up in the center of the room. Shining with freshly applied pigment, the strange design seemed full of light—just stones . . . great blocks piled one upon another, blotting out the sky. But there was nothing monotonous about the composition. Jan had painted it with tenderness and a skillful use of color, so that each stone had a separate identity and a strange rainbow transparency; yet the solidity and unity of the wall remained; but with an added indefinable dimension. On the winding path in the foreground a small human figure stood with arms uplifted, as if in supplication or adoration. Even in that moment of preoccupation Susan knew that it was good. Hurriedly, inadequately, she said so.

Jan looked a little dashed. "Don't you like it very much? Is it a bit too obscure do you think? I wasn't altogether sure about the figure in the foreground. . . ."

"No, Jan, it's wonderful: all of it—absolutely right. But I can't give my mind to it just now." Susan drew in a quick sharp breath. "Something has happened . . . can you stand a bit of shock?" How clumsily she was doing it!

She saw Jan change color. "What sort of a shock? If it's about Tony marrying Sandra Trent, I know. I went into the kitchen just now and found that evening paper you brought home. . . ." Her voice shook piteously, and her eyes filled with tears. She dashed them away angrily with the back of her hand. "Silly to feel like this about it after all this time! But I've been dreading it . . . knowing it had to come. In a way it's a relief. Like having the death sentence confirmed!" She gave a small hollow laugh.

A death sentence! So that's what Tony's marriage to Sandra would have meant to her. Once more Susan had to hastily rearrange her ideas. "Darling, there isn't a death sentence . . . I mean, Tony isn't going to marry Sandra.

That newspaper paragraph is all a mistake." Blunderingly, rapidly, she poured out the whole story seeing Jan go whiter and whiter, her eyes larger and larger.

"Tony is there in the office with father," Susan ended it breathlessly. "Everything is clear to him again—your journey together to Edinburgh, his love for you. He's longing for you, Jan—waiting for you. And the most amazing thing of all is that father sent me to tell you so!"

It was as if a signal long awaited had at last been received. With a low cry, Jan pushed past Susan and ran out of the studio door across the garden. The look on her face at that moment was something Susan would never forget—a blaze of hope, of love . . . of life suddenly restored. Never for Iain could she have looked like this!

Feeling limp and drained, Susan leaned against the studio door. What a day it had been! Tony and Jan and her father reconciled, and Sandra Trent ignominiously banished from the scene. But it served her right, cold-bloodedly using Tony's mental condition to trick him into marrying her. Could anything be more despicable? *She must have been pretty desperately in love*, Susan thought in extenuation. Was she suffering tonight, guessing Tony was hotfoot on his way to Jan? But Susan couldn't bring herself to care. It was the thought of what today's development must do to Iain that now filled her mind. Jan's happiness would mean suffering for him, as well as for Sandra Trent—and it would be through no fault of his own.

In an absent way she began closing the studio windows. She'd better lock up for the night, she thought. Jan would be far too preoccupied to come back to see to it. Automatically she moved around, picking up paint rags, stubs of charcoal, a squashed tube of veridian. The floor could do with a good sweep, she decided. Why were all ar-

tists so untidy? They always seemed to work best in a state
of wild disorder. Susan glanced in despair at the littered
table beside the easel—and her heart gave a sickening jerk.
Iain's card was lying half-stuck to a paint-encrusted
palette. With some idea of salvaging it, she tore it free, and
before she had realized what she was doing she had absorbed its contents. They were brief and to the point. Iain
was arriving in London on Monday for a few days and
would be staying at the Adelphi Hotel.

"If it's okay with your people I could run down to
Moorings on the weekend," he went on. Perhaps it was
because her own name leaped out at her then that Susan
continued reading. "Tell Susan I'll be phoning her at her
office. I hope she'll come out to dinner with me one evening . . . that is if she hasn't anything better to do." A
polite message to Dr. and Mrs. Harrowby followed, a further eager reference to the weekend visit. And that was all.

Susan found herself trembling idiotically as she put the
postcard back on the table. She was ashamed of the waves
of joy that surged over her. But the mere thought of seeing
Iain again—in any circumstances, however unpromis-
ing—swept away all her carefully built-up defenses. And
he wanted to take her out to dinner. Not that there was
anything very extraordinary in that, Susan told herself
hastily. He'd be at a loose end in the evenings after the
business at the show was done . . . would mildly enjoy her
company. In his own way he was fond of her, she knew,
and had always found her a good listener. In fact he had
once told her it was her main asset!

Her thoughts came up with a jerk. In the first flush of
delight she had almost forgotten Jan and Tony. Would
Iain have heard of their reunion before she met him? It
would cast a shadow over their evening together. Seeing

him suffering, disappointed and hiding the pain of his shattered hopes was going to be almost more than she could bear.

"What am I going to say to Iain about you and Tony?" she asked, when Jan told her about Iain's postcard a little later on that amazing Saturday evening. They had all had sherry in the drawing room, Dr. Harrowby apologizing because he couldn't produce the champagne the occasion demanded. But Jan and Tony, side by side on the settee, hardly knew what they were drinking. In the middle of the small celebration, Mrs. Harrowby had returned from her rummage sale, disheveled and exhausted, to be greeted by the astonishing spectacle of Tony restored to their midst, and the doctor calmly accepting him.

There had been explanations, laughter—a joyful incoherent outpouring, Jan and Tony and the doctor all talking at once. It was some time before Mrs. Harrowby, partly restored by a glass of their best Tio Pepe, stooped to kiss Jan's transfigured face. "I'm so glad, darling," she said simply. "It has been an unhappy time for all of us these past weeks. We haven't enjoyed seeing our little girl so sad and subdued."

She turned to Tony, who stood at her side. He put out his hands to her. "Is there a kiss for me, too?" he asked disarmingly. "You know, I've never had a mother as long as I remember—she died when I was born."

"No, Tony, I didn't know. I'm . . . sorry!" Mrs. Harrowby said with an audible sob and took him into her warm embrace, and Susan said shakily from her perch on the arm of her father's chair, "You'll have us all crying in a moment. What about another drink?"

And now she and Jan were upstairs in Jan's room. She was getting ready to go out to dinner with Tony, her lovely face quivering with the joy she couldn't hide. In an off-hand way she had suddenly recalled Iain's message to Susan. "He'll be phoning you up one day next week," she said.

"And when I see him what am I to tell him about you?" Susan persisted.

"Tell him everything . . . just as it happened," Jan returned absently.

"It is going to hurt him terribly, Jan!" Susan protested.

Jan paused in the midst of putting the final touches to her makeup. "Why ever should it? He'll be delighted."

Susan stared at her. "But . . . he's in love with you, Jan. Haven't you realized that all along?"

Apparently she hadn't and dismissed the suggestion now with a great gust of laughter. "You've got an outsized imagination, Sue. Iain has been a wonderful friend to me all through these ghastly weeks . . . letting me write to him about my painting. But there hasn't been any romance in it. It was all far too comfortable for that." She laughed again. "A nice brotherly shoulder to weep on . . . that's what Iain has been to me, and I'm quite certain he never wanted to be anything else."

How could she be so blind! Incredulously, Susan watched her turn to run from the room, her only thought for Tony waiting impatiently for her downstairs.

On Sunday evening Susan went back to London. There had been no opportunity to speak to Jan about Iain again. She had returned late from her dinner with Tony, and first thing on Sunday morning they had set off by car for a long day in the country, saying they would probably have lunch somewhere by the sea. Before they got back Susan had to leave . . . without having made certain that Jan would write the news of her approaching marriage to Iain at his hotel. Supposing she didn't? *How am I going break it to him,* Susan wondered in rising panic, and in the days that followed she waited for his call, her heart filled with longing and apprehension.

CHAPTER THIRTEEN

IAIN DIDN'T TELEPHONE until Wednesday. Susan found it difficult to concentrate on her work. Never had the affairs of Timber Imports Ltd. seemed more boring or old Mr. Digby so tiresome. Every time the phone on her desk rang she would snatch at the receiver eagerly, only to be met with some fatuous inquiry about shipping dates or bills of lading.

But at last it was Iain. At the sound of his warm deep voice, with its Highland lilt, her heart missed a beat, and then to make up for lost time began racing foolishly. Was he really as pleased as he seemed to be when she said, yes, she could have dinner with him that evening? They could meet at his hotel, Susan suggested. "That is, if it is the Adelphi in the Cromwell Road," she added. "It's quite near my apartment."

"I know," he answered, and added, astonishingly, "I've been walking around Cromwell Gardens every evening, looking at your apartment house, wondering which of the lighted windows was yours."

"Why didn't you ring my bell?" Susan asked, thinking privately that he must indeed have been hard up for evening diversion.

"I thought you might be busy," he offered lamely. There was an awkward little pause. What he really meant was that he had doubted the propriety of calling on her in her bed-sitter, Susan decided with an inward smile. In one of their conversations at Glenelg, she remembered, she had confessed to him that the grandly named London "flatlet" consisted of no more than one all-purpose room.

"I'll be with you at seven, then," she promised, and had to hang up abruptly as old Mr. Digby appeared.

Somehow she got through the intervening hours. The day seemed endless, and she kept making silly typing mistakes and having to rip pages out of the machine and begin them all over again. But at last it was five o'clock. When she got back to the apartment she had a bath to steady her idiotic nerves, and put on her prettiest dress—a sapphire blue jersey silk she had recently bought for theater going and club socials. Her new winter coat was a light tweed with blue flecks to match the dress, and it had a big soft fur collar that framed her face becomingly . . . quite glamorous enough for a dinner engagement. Surveying the effect in the mirror Susan decided that that particular deep sapphire was definitely her color—it brought out the gray in her eyes, and did all the right things to her blond hair and fair skin. But she was a little startled at the transfigured expression on her face . . . all lighted up and ecstatic. The way Jan looked when she was running to meet Tony! She'd have to be on her guard this evening, Susan told herself . . . keep her crazy happiness to herself. Composing her features to a more suitable decorum, she set off for the hotel.

Iain was waiting for her in the foyer. He was wearing a dark lounge suit, which made him appear a little unfamiliar. Hungrily she scanned his lean, weather-tanned face. There were deep lines between his brows that she hadn't remembered and he seemed a little tense and strung-up. But there was nothing half-hearted about his wide grin of welcome. He caught both her hands in his own. "You're looking bonny, Susan!"

She couldn't answer him for a moment—just stood there glowing at him, forgetting all about her resolve to keep a poker face.

"My, but it's good to see you again!" The grip of his fingers tightened, squeezing her hands so hard that it hurt.

"And it's good to see you, Iain," she echoed inadequately. "How is Kirstie?"

"Oh, fine, just fine. She sent you a section of honey . . . and some eggs. They are away in my room upstairs. I'll get them for you after dinner. Where would you like to eat, I wonder?" he ran on with oddly nervous haste. "There's a wee place in Knightsbridge that might be all right. The food is good and it's quiet . . . or so I'm told. A chap at the show today recommended it." He was ushering her through the swinging doors as he spoke.

"I'm sure I'll love it," Susan assured him. It would be all the same to her if he took her to a cabdriver's shelter! Just to be here at his side, walking down the Cromwell Road through the misty evening was almost too much bliss to bear. Everything suddenly looked so beautiful—the lights, the shops, the shadowy plane trees, dropping golden, heart-shaped leaves at their feet. There was a scent of late autumn—almost a country smell, bonfires and dampness and the tangy fragrance of the dying leaves.

At the end of the road Iain hailed a taxi. "We could quite well have gone by bus," Susan pointed out frugally. But he handed her into the cab with a lordly air.

"Do you think I'd let you ride in a bus tonight?" he protested as he got in beside her. "This is a special occasion! I don't often have the chance of taking you out."

Her heart sank a little. Quite obviously he didn't know

about Jan and Tony. He wouldn't be so cheerful if he did. *Really Jan ought to have written or phoned him before now*, Susan thought with a twinge of impatience. But she seemed so obtuse about the whole situation—so serenely unaware of Iain's feelings for her.

"How are things at Moorings?" he was asking.

Susan drew in a sharp breath. She'd tell him right away here in the dark of the taxi, she decided. It would give him a minute or two to recover some semblance of composure before they reached the restaurant. She said slowly, deliberately, giving it to him all in one sharp cruel blow—because she felt that was the way it would be easiest for him, "Things are pretty hectic at Moorings just now, with Jan's wedding in the offing."

"I know," he answered lightly. "It's terrific, isn't it? Everything worked out for her in the end! But somehow I had a hunch that it would."

She stared at his shadowy profile, dumbfounded. If he was putting on an act, it was a pretty convincing one. "Jan wrote to you?" she asked.

"No, she told me over the phone. I'd phoned up to arrange about the weekend, and there she was all bubbling over with the good news."

"The wedding is to be almost at once," Susan pursued relentlessly. "Tony is anxious to get back to Paris and catch up on neglected work."

"So I gathered. Jan must be up to her eyes in preparations . . . far too busy to entertain a stray weekend guest, though I knew she'd deny it if I put it to her. So I tactfully told her I had to go back to Glenelg on the night express on Friday." Did she catch the ghost of a regretful sigh, Susan wondered.

"I'd only be in the way now," he said. "Done out of my

job as comforter-in-chief!'' he laughed briefly, bitterly, or
so it seemed to Susan, keyed up to catch every telltale in-
flection. For a moment she wondered if she might persuade him to come to Moorings in spite of the looming
wedding. Even if Jan was busy she, herself, would be
there. But he wouldn't, she reflected sadly, find it much
fun being paired off with her—as a doubtful second best.
And it would be hard for him to see Jan and Tony in their
newly recaptured happiness. Brave as he was being about
it, he wasn't quite brave enough for that.

The restaurant when they arrived proved to be all Iain
had hoped—small, intimate, with rose-shaded lighting.
They sat in a secluded corner in an alcove discreetly hidden
by potted palms. Quite obviously planned for lovers,
Susan thought wryly.

Soft-footed waiters came and went, doing mysterious
things with chafing dishes over burning flames at a little
side table—the decorous ritual of haute cuisine. And Iain,
she discovered, was surprisingly knowledgeable in ordering
exotic dishes. But he had lived for his two years of soldier-
ing on the Mediterranean seaboard, she remembered.

"Did you learn to eat kabob in Nicosia?" she asked
him, when the skewered mixed grill in its bed of savory rice
and tiny green peas appeared. They talked for a while of
his experiences in Cyprus. A safely remote topic, Susan
felt, but as soon as she could she switched the conversation
to Glenelg.

There were so many questions she was hungering to ask.
He'd had a bumper crop of tomatoes, he told her. Kirstie
had bottled dozens of jars for sale. And his Christmas
chrysanthemums were coming along fine. Jake, the young
pedigree sheep dog, had arrived.

"I wish you could see him when I put him through his

paces," Iain said. "It's quite something to watch these dogs at work. And Jake is outstanding. I'm thinking of entering him for the sheep-dog trials in the spring."

"Oh, Iain, how I'd love to be there!" Susan burst out with such naked longing in her tone, that he gave her a mildly startled glance.

"You sound as if you really mean that," he marveled.

Why did he have to seem so absurdly gratified? "Of course I mean it!" She dropped her lashes to hide the hunger in her eyes. "Spring must be such a beautiful time in the Lowlands."

"It is, " he agreed flatly and left it there—not suggesting she should run up and have a look at it, which she could easily manage at Easter when she had five days holiday from the office.

There was a small empty silence while she waited for the invitation that didn't come.

"How is Tibby?" she asked at last, smothering her disappointment.

"Fatter and lazier than ever," Iain laughed. "We've had to import a couple of working cats from a neighboring farm to keep down the rats in the barn. And now that's enough of Glenelg and its doings . . . let's hear about you for a change. What have you been up to since you got back to town? Have you been to any shows or concerts?"

"Oh, yes, indeed!" She tried to make it sound enthusiastic, but somehow the autumn concerts and theaters had fallen oddly flat this year. "There was a wonderful Beethoven night at the Albert Hall," she said. "And a friend of mine managed to get tickets for the recital of that new Russian pianist—Malinin. Then there was the last night at the proms, of course."

"I know," Iain nodded. "I listened to it on our radio. It was the usual cheerful, noisy affair."

They had reached the coffee stage now and she had noticed him glance surreptitiously at his watch. Soon he would be asking for the bill. The evening was almost over. It had gone so quickly! *I ought not to have come,* Susan thought. Just to see Iain for a few hours like this was worse than not seeing him at all. It was going to take her a long while to get back to the precarious peace she had achieved—the dulled ache of resignation. A queer cold panic filled her heart. "Won't you change your mind and come down to Moorings for the weekend after all?" she found herself pleading.

His jawline hardened. "I don't think I'd better, Susan. It's very kind of you. But in the circumstances . . . ." He left the unfinished sentence in the air. A leaden silence fell on them . . . the small glow of companionship that had carried them through the meal was suddenly gone. Iain couldn't pretend any longer. His gallant facade of unconcern had collapsed.

If only he knew how well I understand what he is going through at this moment, Susan thought. She looked into his darkly burning eyes and was shocked at the anguish that looked back at her.

"I'm sorry, Iain!" she found herself saying brokenly, impulsively. "I'd have given anything if . . . things could have turned out differently for you."

She saw him wince painfully. "So you guessed how it was with me . . . those days at Glenelg!" He gave a short hard laugh. "I'd no idea I was being so transparent! I didn't mean to be."

"You weren't transparent," she offered hurriedly. "It was . . . just that I knew!"

"They say women always do," he murmured cryptically. "Must be a lot of fun for them!" His lips curled as though the words had a bitter taste.

"Fun!" Susan echoed in a puzzled tone. "Nothing that hurt you could be fun for me, Iain." A tremor passed over his face—it made him look very young and vulnerable.

"I know, Sue. I shouldn't have said that." He slid a conciliatory hand over her own and looked into her troubled eyes. "Don't worry. I'll weather it. Worse things happen at sea!" And then as if he'd had enough of this rather trying exchange, he turned abruptly, summoned a hovering waiter and demanded the bill.

"Let's walk," Susan suggested, when they left the restaurant. "It's not all that far and it's such a lovely night." A taxi would get them back far too quickly, was what she really meant.

They went at a leisurely pace past the brightly lighted windows of the great closed stores. Now and then they stopped to admire the dazzling displays—clothes, cars, antiques. It was as if they were both reluctant to bring the evening to an end. A window set out to represent a glittering stream-lined kitchen caught Susan's attention.

"A bit more up-to-date than the kitchen at Glenelg with its clumsy old iron range," Iain remarked dourly.

"But not half so cosy," Susan said loyally. "I often think of it, with its gay rag rugs and geraniums. And it has far more space than any modern kitchen. The jam making sessions were such fun!" She ended on a long quivering sigh.

"All the same," Iain said with a nod at the glittering window, "I wouldn't mind betting this is the sort of kitchen you'll choose when you marry and set up housekeeping—a fridge and a washing machine and a marvelous electric stove with thermostat control and a kettle that whistles 'God Save the Queen' when it comes to the boil."

Susan laughed aloud at this flight of fancy. "If my husband can afford it," she went on with the make-believe game. "Have you any idea, my poor innocent, what all those pretty gadgets would cost? A kitchen of that sort would run into a cool five hundred pounds."

Iain questioned the figure. They argued about it mildly until they reached the turning into Cromwell Gardens. Then a strained silence fell between them. This time when they said "goodbye" it would most likely be for good, Susan thought desperately. It was no moment for false pride. Somehow, she must see Iain again before he returned to Scotland. "What time does your train leave on Friday?" she asked.

"Around about midnight," he answered, as she had guessed he might. That late express with its sleepers was the obvious choice for an all night journey north. On several occasions she had booked a berth on it for Mr. Digby—when he had gone to visit their branch office at Newcastle.

"You'll have Friday evening clear, then," she pointed out. "If you aren't doing anything else, would you care to come to a concert with me? I've got a spare ticket for the Isaac Stern recital at the Wigmore Hall."

Iain hesitated. In the light of the streetlights his face looked strangely drawn. "That's nice of you, Susan. I can't think of anything I'd like better . . . but oughtn't you to keep the tickets for your . . . friend? It was good of him to spare you to me this evening."

She turned to him in blankest bewilderment. "My friend!"

"The man you are going to marry. Kirstie told me about him." He broke off, seeing her look of shocked astonishment. "Hope I'm not speaking out of turn . . . but Kirstie didn't seem to think it was a secret. . . ."

She made a small baffled gesture. "But I don't

understand! Kirstie told you I was engaged to be married?'' All of a sudden light dawned . . . that Sunday evening of aching jealousy when she and Kirstie had watched Iain and Jan set out for a walk up Hopes Valley!

Susan gave a small shamed laugh. ''It isn't true, Iain! It was the silliest misunderstanding. I'd forgotten all about it until this moment. It was that Sunday you took Jan up Hopes Valley to see the reservoir. Kirstie and I got to talking about love . . . and so on, and half-jokingly she said she guessed I was surrounded with dozens of eligible boyfriends in London, and in the same flippant tone I agreed that I was. When she asked if there was one special 'eligible'—I more or less said there was—to . . . save my pride.'' Her voice dropped to a whisper. ''The whole thing started, you see, because she was disappointed you had fallen in love with Jan . . . instead of me. It wasn't very tactful of her . . . and it . . . annoyed me rather.''

Iain stopped short in his tracks and gripped her arm. ''Look! Am I going crazy?'' he demanded. ''What was that you said just now—about Kirstie thinking I was in love with Jan?''

''We both thought it,'' Susan said. Her heart felt as if it were falling down a steep flight of stairs, and her breath was all tangled up in her throat.

''But, Susan . . . ?'' His grip on her arm tightened painfully. ''Was that what you meant when you told me tonight you guessed how I felt? Was it that you thought I was pining in my unrequited love for young Jan?''

She gave a shaky, inarticulate nod.

''But, good heavens, Susan . . . !'' He took his hand from her arm and stood back, surveying her as if she were some extraordinary apparition. Consternation and incredulity distorted his thin brown face. ''What sort of a fool have I been?'' he demanded angrily. "How on earth could I have given you that impression?''

"It seemed so . . . inevitable,'' Susan faltered. "Jan is so attractive. . . . You said yourself she was a heart wrecker. And you were so kind to her . . . so concerned for her. . . .''

"Only because I was sorry for her,'' Iain burst out. "But there was never anything more than that in my mind. There couldn't have been. I was so taken up with you. . . .'' A dull red crept up under his tan and his eyes weren't angry anymore. "It was always you, Susan,'' he offered brokenly. "Right from the day we traveled up from London together.''

Weakly she leaned against a convenient area railing. "Why didn't you tell me?'' she heard herself ask in a small strange voice that didn't seem to belong to her.

"I tried to,'' Iain confessed. "But I hadn't the gall to believe you could ever bother about me. Glenelg is so different from the kind of life you are accustomed to. I couldn't imagine you settling down to our countrified, rather isolated way of living. Then Kirstie told me about this chap in London.''

"There's no chap in London,'' Susan echoed foolishly.

"So you are . . . free!'' he marveled. "Heart-whole . . . ?''

She lifted her pale, illuminated face. "Not heart-whole, Iain,'' she whispered. "Not since that day you caught me by the shoulders and pulled me into the Caledonian Express.''

"Susan!'' He took her small cold hands and gathered her into his arms. She buried her face against his shoulder. It was as if she were drowning in a great roaring triumphant sea. There were no clear thoughts in her mind anymore—only a sense of immeasurable relief. After the pain and frustration of the evening, the long lonely weeks of nagging heartache, it was almost more than she could bear. A deep sob shook her.

"You're crying, darling!" He put a hand under her chin and forced her to raise her tear-wet face.

"Only because I'm so happy, Iain . . . and because we've both been so . . . silly!" She gave a small hysterical laugh.

"Oh, Susan, Susan!" was all he could say. . . . Taking a handkerchief from his pocket he dried her wet lashes, then very gently he kissed her on the brow. "I can't believe it!" he marveled.

"Neither can I!" Susan sighed.

An elderly lady exercising a poodle passed them with a disapproving averted head.

"Can we go upstairs to your apartment and talk about it?" Iain ventured. "This square seems to be full of old ladies and dogs—and I want to kiss you . . . properly!"

Only then did Susan realize she was leaning against the railing of her own apartment house. It was awkward fumbling for her key in her bag with Iain's arm so tightly around her and still more awkward getting up the three flights of stairs. But somehow they made it. She wished she had left her room a little more tidy—filled it with flowers. It ought to be hung with green lilac boughs, she thought wildly, strewn with rose petals.

"I'll make us some coffee," she said nervously.

"No, you won't," Iain declared in a masterful voice. "We've just had coffee." He sat on the edge of the wide divan and pulled her down beside him. "We've wasted enough time," he pleaded softly. "We've so much to catch up on . . . oh, Susan, my darling, my love!" When he kissed her this time it was full on her quivering lips. Hungrily they clung to one another. The small shabby room dissolved around them. In that timeless movment of dawning love the whole world was theirs—and all heaven.

"I suppose this really *is* happening to us!" Susan whispered presently. "I feel I want to keep pinching myself to be sure I'm not dreaming!"

"So do I!" Iain marveled. "It's a bit much to take in all at once. And the amazing thing is we've got the rest of our lives to sort it out. . . . Oh, Susan, think of it!"

It was later, much later, when coherence returned, that they managed to get down to concrete plans. Iain would not now go back to Scotland on Friday night. He would have his weekend at Moorings after all. "I'll have to put in an appearance," he pointed out, "to talk to that formidable father of yours."

"But he likes you, Iain," Susan assured him. "And he's not really formidable."

"He may be when he hears I want to marry you as soon as possible. Can you think of any good reason why we should wait?"

"Right now," Susan said dreamily, "I can't think of anything, but how much I love you."

"A very proper state of mind!" Iain laughed.

"Darling!" Susan said happily. "You sound so conceited all at once. I had no idea you were like this."

"Of course I'm conceited!" he exulted. "Who in my shoes wouldn't be? To think that you love me, Susan! It makes me the proudest man on earth."

But it was a very humble and adoring face he lifted to her, as she drew away from him and stood up—saying she was going to make that coffee after all. "I think we need it by now!"

He watched her put the kettle on the gas ring to boil, insisted upon helping her set out the cups and saucers and biscuits on a tray. It was while they were drinking the coffee side by side on the divan that Iain said musingly. "Do you think you could be ready to be married the same day as Jan and Tony? Wouldn't a double wedding save a lot of bother . . . and be rather fun?"

"The same thought *had* passed through my mind," Susan admitted. There was a moment of stunned, incredulous silence while they savored the miracle. A wedding date already as good as fixed.

"Oh, Iain!" Susan sighed ecstatically.

"Oh, Susan!" he echoed.

They put their cups hastily down on the floor, and by the time they remembered them again the coffee was stone cold.

HARLEQUIN CLASSIC LIBRARY

Great old romance classics from our
early publishing lists.

FREE BONUS BOOK

On the following page is a coupon with which
you may order any or all of these titles. If you
order all nine, you will receive a FREE book—
Nurses Are People, a heartwarming classic
romance by Lucy Agnes Hancock.

The fourth set of nine novels in the
HARLEQUIN CLASSIC LIBRARY

Great old favorites...
Harlequin Classic Library

Complete and mail this coupon today!

Harlequin Reader Service

In U.S.A.
MPO Box 707
Niagara Falls, N Y 14302

In Canada
649 Ontario St.
Stratford, Ontario N5A 6W2

Please send me the following novels from the Harlequin Classic Library. I am enclosing my check or money order for $1.25 for each novel ordered, plus 59¢ to cover postage and handling. If I order all nine titles, I will receive a FREE book, *Nurses Are People*, by Lucy Agnes Hancock.

☐ 28   ☐ 31   ☐ 34
☐ 29   ☐ 32   ☐ 35
☐ 30   ☐ 33   ☐ 36

Number of novels checked @ $1.25 each =	$_____
N.Y. and Ariz. residents add appropriate sales tax	$_____
Postage and handling	$_____ .59
TOTAL	$_____

I enclose _____
(Please send check or money order. We cannot be responsible for cash sent through the mail.)
Prices subject to change without notice.

Name _____
(Please Print)

Address _____

City _____

State/Prov. _____

Zip/Postal Code _____

Offer expires July 31, 1981.   101566876